THE BEST GIFT

IRENE HANNON

Steeple
Hill®

Published by Steeple Hill Books™

STEEPLE HILL BOOKS

Steeple
Hill®

ISBN 0-373-87302-6

THE BEST GIFT

Copyright © 2005 by Irene Hannon

This edition published by arrangement with Steeple Hill Books.

® and TM are trademarks of Steeple Hill Books, used under license.
Trademarks indicated with ® are registered in the United States Patent
and Trademark Office, the Canadian Trade Marks Office and in other
countries.

www.SteepleHill.com

Printed in U.S.A.

A.J. glanced at the tall man who was looking at her with resignation.

Was this Blake Sullivan? If so, he sure didn't match the image she'd created in her mind. She'd envisioned a bookish type, fiftyish, possibly balding, sporting a paunch. A fussy, precise and stern curmudgeon.

She'd been dead wrong about the physical description. Blake was tall, with dark brown hair and intense cobalt-blue eyes. His crisp oxford shirt, beige slacks and well-polished leather shoes bordered on being preppy. His attire also showed off his athletic build.

A.J. could only imagine how she appeared, standing there dripping rainwater on the hardwood floor of the bookstore, her hair no doubt plastered to her head. She could read enough from the look in his eyes. So much for first impressions.

"I'm looking for Blake Sullivan."

Blake waited a moment, as if trying to decide what to do. Finally he approached her. "You've found him."

She extended her hand. "I'm A. J. Williams. Your new partner."

Books by Irene Hannon

Steeple Hill Love Inspired

IRENE HANNON

is an award-winning author who has been a writer for as long as she can remember. She "officially" launched her career at the age of ten, when she was one of the winners in a "complete-the-story" contest conducted by a national children's magazine. More recently, Irene won the coveted RITA® Award for her 2002 Love Inspired *Never Say Goodbye*. Irene, who spent many years in an executive corporate communications position with a Fortune 500 company, now devotes herself full-time to her writing career. In her "spare" time, she enjoys performing in community musical theater productions, singing in the church choir, gardening, cooking and spending time with family and friends. She and her husband, Tom—whom she describes as "my own romantic hero"—make their home in Missouri.

The Lord is near. Have no anxiety, but in every
prayer and supplication with thanksgiving
let your petitions be made known to God.
—*Philippians* 4:5–6

To my darling niece, Maureen Elizabeth,
who came early to claim our hearts with her
sunny smile. We love you, snowflake!

Prologue

Morgan Williams glanced impatiently at her watch, then gave an exasperated sigh. "I wish he'd hurry. I have a plane to catch."

A.J. turned from the window, which framed a row of flame-red maples against a brilliant St. Louis late-October sky. "Chill out, Morgan," she said wryly. "The advertising world can live without you for a few more hours."

Morgan gave her younger sister an annoyed look as she rummaged in her purse for her cell phone. "Trust me, A.J. The business arena is nothing like your nonprofit world. Hours do matter to us. So do minutes."

"More's the pity," A.J. responded, turning back to admire the view again. "Life is too short to be so stressed about things as fleeting as ad campaigns."

Morgan opened her mouth to respond, but Clare beat her to it. "Don't you think we should put our philosophical differences aside today, out of respect for Aunt Jo?" she interjected gently.

Morgan and A.J. turned in unison toward their older sister, and A.J. grinned.

"Ever the peacemaker, Clare," she said, her voice tinged with affection.

Clare smiled. "Somebody had to keep the two of you from doing each other bodily harm when we were growing up. And since I was the only one who didn't inherit Mom's McCauley-red hair—and the temper that went with it—I suppose the job had to fall to me."

A.J. joined Morgan on the couch. "Okay. In honor of Aunt Jo, I declare a truce. How about it, Morgan?"

Morgan hesitated, then tucked her cell phone in her purse. "Truce," she agreed with a grin. "Besides, much as I hate to admit that my kid sister is sometimes right, I am occasionally guilty of taking my job too seriously."

"Occasionally?" A.J. rolled her eyes.

"Enough, you two," Clare admonished with a smile.

A.J. laughed. "Okay, okay. You must whip those kids into shape whenever you substitute teach. In a nice way, of course. Their regular teacher is probably astounded at their good behavior when she gets back."

Clare's smile faded, and she looked down to fiddle with the strap on her purse. "I do my best. But I still have a lot to learn. It's been so many years since I taught…it's harder some days than others."

A.J. and Morgan exchanged a look. "Hang in there, Clare," Morgan encouraged. "We're here for you."

"It does get easier. Not overnight. But bit by bit.

Trust me," A.J. added, her own voice suddenly a bit uneven.

Clare blinked rapidly several times before she looked up. "Sorry. I usually have my emotions better under control. I guess Aunt Jo's memorial service today just brought back…a lot of memories."

Her voice caught on the last word, and A.J. and Morgan simultaneously reached for their sister's hands. Clare gazed down and took a deep breath. "A circle of love," she said softly.

"The three musketeers," A.J. added, using one of their childhood nicknames as she grasped Morgan's hand to complete the circle.

Morgan squeezed both hands. "One for all, all for one."

Suddenly the door to the inner-office opened, and the sisters dropped their hands as they all turned toward attorney Seth Mitchell.

For a long moment the distinguished, gray-haired man standing in the doorway studied Jo Warren's three great-nieces, taking full advantage of the opportunity to examine them up close rather than from a distance, as he had at the service this morning. He was pleased to note that none flinched at his unhurried perusal.

A.J. was tall and lean, with long, naturally curly strawberry blond hair, too unruly to be tamed even by strategically placed combs. She seemed perfectly comfortable in her somewhat eclectic attire—a calf-length skirt and a long tunic top, cinched at the waist with an unusual metal belt—and looked at him with genuine curiosity, as if the current situation was immensely interesting to her.

Morgan, who wore her dark, copper-colored hair in a sleek, shoulder-length style, was dressed in chic business attire that spelled "big city" and "success." She gave him a somewhat bored, impatient "let's-get-on-with-this-because-I-have-better-things-to-do" look.

Clare, the shortest of the three, wore her honey-gold hair in an elegant chignon that complemented her designer suit and Gucci purse. She had hope in her eyes when she looked at him—as well as a deep and lingering sadness.

Yes, they were just as Jo had described them, Seth concluded. A.J., the free spirit who took an interest in everything around her and was grounded in the here and now…perhaps too much so. Morgan, the somewhat jaded high-powered executive who might need some help straightening out her priorities. And Clare, whose double tragedy had left her in need of both emotional and financial help. Now, more than ever, Jo's legacy made sense to Seth.

He moved forward. "Good morning, ladies. I'm Seth Mitchell. I recognize you from Jo's description—A.J., Morgan, Clare," he said, correctly identifying the sisters as he extended his hand to each in turn. "Please accept my condolences on the loss of your great-aunt. She was a wonderful lady."

They murmured polite responses, and he motioned toward his office. "If you're ready, we can proceed with the reading of the will."

He didn't speak again until they were all seated, at which point he picked up a hefty document. "I'll give each of you a copy of your great-aunt's will to take with you, so I don't think there's any reason to go through this whole document now. A lot of it is legalese, and there are some charitable bequests that you can review at your leisure. I thought we could restrict the formal reading to the section that affects each of you directly, if that's agreeable."

"Absolutely," Morgan replied. "Besides, my plane for Boston leaves in less than three hours. I know Clare needs to get back to Kansas City, and A.J. has a long drive to Chicago."

Seth looked at the other two sisters. When they nodded their assent, he flipped through the document to a marked page and began to read.

"Insofar as I have no living relatives other than my three great nieces the daughters of my sole nephew, Jonathan Williams, now deceased—I bequeath the bulk of my estate to them, in the following manner and with the following stipulations and conditions.

"To Abigail Jeanette Williams, I bequeath half ownership of my bookstore in St. Louis, Turning Leaves, with the stipulation that she retain ownership for a minimum of six months and work full-time in the store during this period. The remaining half ownership I bequeath to the present manager, Blake Sullivan, with the same stipulation.

"To Morgan Williams, I bequeath half ownership of Serenity Point, my cottage in Seaside, Maine, providing that she retains her ownership for a six-month period following my death and that she spends a total of four weeks in residence at the cottage. During this time she is also to provide advertising and promotional assistance for Good Shepherd Camp and attend board meetings as an advisory member. The remaining half ownership of the cottage I bequeath to Grant Kincaid of Seaside, Maine.

"To Clare Randall, I bequeath my remaining financial assets, except for those designated to be given to the charities specified in this document, with the stipulation that she serve as nanny for Nicole Wright, daughter of Dr. Adam Wright of Hope Creek, North Carolina, for a period of six months, at no charge to Dr. Wright.

"Should the stipulations and conditions for the aforementioned bequests not be fulfilled, the specified assets will be disposed of according to directions given to my attorney, Seth Mitchell. He will also designate the date on which the clock will begin ticking on the six-month period specified in my will. "

Seth lowered the document to his desk and looked at the women across from him. A.J. still looked interested. Morgan looked aggravated. Clare looked uncertain.

"There you have it, ladies. I can provide more details on your bequests to each of you individually, but are there any general questions that I can answer?"

"Well, I might as well write mine off right now," Morgan said in disgust. "There's no way I can be away from the office for four days, let alone four weeks. And what is Good Shepherd Camp?"

"Who is this Dr. Wright?" Clare asked with a frown. "And what makes Aunt Jo think he would want me as a nanny?"

"When can I start?" A.J. asked.

"Let me take your questions and comments one at a time," Seth said. "Morgan, you have the right to turn down the bequest, of course. But I would advise you to get some legal and financial counsel first. Jo bought that property years ago, when Seaside was just a quiet, backwater village. The area is now a bustling tourist mecca. So her property has increased significantly in value. As for how to meet your aunt's residence stipulation—I'm afraid I can't advise you on that. Good Shepherd is a summer camp in Maine for children from troubled homes. Your aunt has been involved with the organization for many years.

"Clare, Dr. Wright is an old friend of Jo's from St. Louis. I believe she met him through her church, and even when he moved to North Carolina, they remained close friends. He's a widower with an eleven-year-old daughter who apparently needs guidance and closer supervision. As to why Jo thought Dr. Wright would be interested in having you as a nanny, I can't say.

"A.J., I'd ask you to give me a couple of weeks to tie up some legalities before you contact Mr. Sullivan. I'll let you know when it's appropriate to call."

He paused and glanced at his desk calendar. "Let's officially start the clock for the six-month period on December 1. That will give you about a month to make plans. Now, are there any more general questions?"

The three women looked at him, looked at each other, then silently shook their heads.

"Very well." He handed them each a manila envelope. "But do feel free to call if any come up as you review the will more thoroughly." He rose, signaling the end of the meeting, and extended his hand to each sister in turn. "Again, my condolences on the death of your great-aunt. Jo had a positive impact on countless lives and will be missed by many people. I know she loved each of you very much, and that she wanted you to succeed in claiming your bequests.

"Good luck, ladies."

Chapter One

It wasn't fair.

Blake Sullivan stared at the letter from Seth Mitchell. How could Jo do this to him? Okay, so maybe she'd never actually promised to leave the entire business to him, but she had certainly implied as much. After all, they'd been friends for twenty-one years. And he'd walked away from a successful career in investment banking three years ago to rescue Turning Leaves, when Jo's waning energy began to affect the business and her ongoing generosity had finally depleted her financial cushion. He'd enjoyed it so much that he'd stayed to turn the sleepy, neighborhood bookshop into a thriving enterprise. Without him, the business would have been bankrupt by now.

And what was his reward for three years of diligent labor on her behalf? She'd left half the business to her flighty, do-gooder great-niece who probably didn't know the difference between a balance sheet and a balance beam.

Blake felt his blood pressure edge up and forced himself to take a slow, deep breath. Getting worked up about the situation wasn't going to change it, he reminded himself. Maybe if he and Jo had had more time to discuss it, things would have turned out differently. But the fast-acting cancer that had struck so suddenly and taken her so quickly had left them little time for business discussions. By the time she'd told anyone about her illness, it was far too late to discuss any succession plans.

Blake fingered the letter from her attorney, a hollow feeling in the pit of his stomach. He could just walk away, of course. Let the business disintegrate in the hands of Jo's inexperienced and probably disinterested heir. But he'd poured too much of himself into the bookshop, cared too much about it to let it die.

Which left him only one option.

And that did not make him happy.

Blake watched the caller ID disappear as the line went dead. Jo's niece again. He couldn't avoid her forever, but he needed more time to think things through. Especially since he'd received Jo's brief, enigmatic letter, which had arrived a couple of days after Seth Mitchell's.

He lifted it from the kitchen counter as he waited for the microwave to reheat the cannelloni from his favorite restaurant on The Hill—a splurge that would wreak havoc with his well-disciplined diet, especially with the Thanksgiving Day triathlon looming on the horizon. But he'd needed a pick-me-up after the news from Seth.

Blake scanned the single sheet of paper once more.

Dear Blake, I know you will be disappointed by my bequest. Please understand that I fully appreciate all you have done these past three years to make Turning Leaves successful, and that my gratitude goes deeper than I can say. I have valued our friendship and our partnership, and one of my great joys has been to watch you grow into a fine man.

At the same time, I feel a special obligation to my nieces. A.J. needs an anchor in her life, and I am hopeful that Turning Leaves will provide that for her. She has been drifting these past few years, for reasons that even she may not fully comprehend, but which you may eventually come to understand. I would consider it a final favor for an old friend if you would help her learn the business we both love. With great affection, Jo.

The beeper went off on the microwave, and Blake retrieved the cannelloni. He didn't understand some of Jo's comments, but he did understand the part about the final favor. And as rational thought had prevailed over the past couple of days, he'd come to acknowledge that as much as he'd done for Jo these past three years, it was he who was deeply in *her* debt.

As he poured a soft drink, he thought back to the summer when he was thirteen. It was a couple of years after Jo's husband died, and she had just opened her shop. Pure chance brought them together. Or fate. Or maybe Providence, if one were religiously inclined. But whatever it was, it had changed his life.

Blake's parents had decided to spend the summer in St. Louis, for reasons Blake couldn't recall. They were always going somewhere on a whim, for a rally or to hang out with friends or simply for a change of scene. Jo had hired his father to do some carpentry and odd jobs at the shop. Blake hadn't known anyone in St. Louis, and after thirteen years he'd learned that it didn't pay to try to make friends in a new town, because in a few weeks or a few months his vagabond parents would be on the road again. So he'd simply tagged along with his father to Jo's. And those had been some of his happiest days.

Jo had taken him under her wing, giving him odd jobs to do and regaling him with stories of her world travels and the exotic places she and her husband had visited. She'd discussed politics with him, and philosophy, as if he were an adult, which did wonders for his shaky thirteen-year-old self-esteem. He owed his love of learning and books to Jo. And so much more. Something about him must have made an impact on her as well, because she'd stayed in touch with him when his family moved on at the end of the summer. He still had her letters tucked in a shoe box in his closet. During his teenage years, she was the one stable person in his unsettled, unpredictable world, and he clung to her voraciously, sharing with her his fears and his hopes. She'd always encouraged him, and when it came time for college, she'd come through for him again, providing a significant amount of the funding for his education.

So even though he'd rescued Turning Leaves, his efforts were small repayment for all she'd been to him.

Friend. Confidante. Supporter. Benefactor. And now she had one last request. Help her great-niece learn the business.

How could he say no?

"Blake, A. J. Williams is on the phone for you."

Blake frowned and transferred his gaze from the computer screen to the flickering phone light.

"Bad time? Should I get a number?"

Slowly, Blake shook his head and looked over at his assistant manager. There was no sense avoiding the inevitable. "No. I'll take it, Nancy. Thanks."

She hesitated at the doorway. "Is everything okay?"

Blake heard the trepidation in her voice, and nodded. "I'm sure everything will be fine."

As a divorced mother with two part-time jobs, Nancy worked hard to provide for herself and her ten-year-old daughter. She'd been unsettled ever since Jo's death, clearly unsure about the future of Turning Leaves. Blake had tried to be reassuring, but he couldn't offer much encouragement since he felt the same way.

Blake looked back at the flashing light. Too bad he hadn't hung around long enough after Jo's memorial service to meet her nieces—and get a few insights about his new partner. He took a deep breath, picked up the receiver and punched the flashing button.

"Blake Sullivan."

"Mr. Sullivan, this is A. J. Williams, Jo Warren's great-niece. I believe you've heard from Seth Mitchell about my aunt's bequest of Turning Leaves?"

The voice was a bit breathless, but bright and friendly. His was cautious and curt. "Yes."

There was a hesitation, as if she expected him to say more. When he didn't, she continued. "Well, I'm getting ready to make travel plans to St. Louis and wanted to talk with you about the timing of my arrival."

Deep inside Blake had harbored a dim hope that A.J. would pass on her inheritance. From the little he'd heard about her through the years, a bookshop didn't seem like the kind of thing she'd be interested in. Now that hope flickered and died. "There's no rush from my end."

His less-than-friendly reply was met with a moment of silence. Okay, maybe his comment wasn't exactly warm and fuzzy. But it was the truth.

"Well, according to Seth Mitchell, the clock starts ticking on December 1. But I see no reason to wait until then. I can wrap things up here pretty quickly."

Now it was his turn to hesitate. But only briefly, because he wanted an answer to his next question. "May I ask you something, Ms. Williams?"

"Yes." Her reply was immediate, but cautious.

"How much interest do you have in Turning Leaves?"

"What do you mean?"

"Is this a lark for you, or do you have a serious interest in the business?"

There was a moment of silence. "Maybe a little of both," she finally said. "I'm ready for a change, and the business sounds interesting. I don't really have any long-term plans."

"Then let me make you a proposition. I happen to care about Turning Leaves. And I do have long-term plans, which revolve around this business. So my proposal is this—I'll work with you for six months so you can claim your inheritance. At that point, you give me the option to buy your half of the business at a mutually agreeable price. That lets us keep Jo's legacy alive, and frees you to pursue your next…lark."

On the other end of the line, A.J. felt the stirrings of her Irish temper. This man was treating her like some irresponsible airhead who flitted from one distraction to another. She hardly considered her years in Afghanistan, nor the past two working in Good Samaritan, Inc. headquarters, a "lark." Nor the rigorous years of training that went into earning her M.D.A. She didn't like his inference one bit. In fact, she didn't think she liked Blake Sullivan. But she didn't have to, she reminded herself. She just had to work with him for six months. And she'd had plenty of experience working under difficult conditions with difficult people. Maybe Mr. Sullivan would even discover that she wasn't quite as capricious and flighty as he seemed to think. Starting right now. Because she wasn't about to make any promises for anything six months down the road. That was a lifetime. And a lot of things could happen between now and then.

When she spoke again, her voice was brisk and businesslike. "I'll tell you what, Mr. Sullivan. I'll agree to consider your proposal when the time comes. But I can't make any promises. I might decide to stay on at Turning Leaves. However, if I do decide to sell, I would certainly give you first consideration."

Blake frowned at the unexpected response. Her tone had cooled considerably, and he couldn't blame her. He hadn't exactly been friendly. And he couldn't argue with her counterproposal. He would have offered the same thing. So it appeared he was stuck with Jo's niece for the next six months. Unless he just walked away. But he couldn't do that. Not after pouring himself into the business for the past three years. Yet could he stand by and watch it potentially falter in the hands of an inexperienced and seemingly strong-willed partner? For once in his life he wished he was a praying man, because he sure could use some guidance.

While Blake considered her counteroffer, A.J. did pray. Because she needed the bookshop. And she needed Blake, with his years of experience, to help her run it. Though she loved her work at Good Samaritan, the spartan pay in a high cost of living city like Chicago made it more and more difficult for her to keep up with daily expenses. She had known for several months that she'd have to make a change. The options were simple: Stay in Chicago and find a better-paying job, or move on to something—and someplace—entirely new. After praying, she'd been leaning toward the latter option. So when Jo's legacy had fallen in her lap, she had seen it almost as divine intervention, a reaffirmation of her decision to pack up and move on. And even if she decided to sell after six months, the legacy would give her a financial cushion to fund whatever direction her life took.

"All right, Ms. Williams. I'll accept your terms. If you could put them in a letter to me, I'd appreciate it."

"You have my word."

"In the business world, it's better to have things in writing."

He could hear anger nipping at the edges of her voice when she spoke. "Fine. I'll put something in the mail today. Would you like it notarized as well?"

He ignored the touch of sarcasm in her tone. "That won't be necessary. When are you planning to come down?"

"I have to close up my apartment and give notice at my job. In a couple of weeks, probably. I'll call ahead to let you know my plans. And feel free to call me in the interim if you need anything."

"I think we'll be just fine."

Without you.

The words were unspoken. But the implication came through loud and clear.

Three hours.

A.J. was three hours late.

Blake glanced at his watch for the umpteenth time and shook his head in exasperation.

"I'm sure she'll be here soon," Nancy said as she passed by with a stack of books to restock a display. "It's such a nasty day out…maybe the weather delayed her."

As if to reinforce her comment, a crash of thunder shook the building.

Blake wasn't buying it. "For three hours? Hardly likely. She probably forgot what time she said she was going to arrive."

Nancy looked at him curiously as she arranged the

books. "Boy, you sure formed a strong impression of her from a couple of phone conversations. It's not like you to make snap judgments."

He shrugged stiffly. "Well, let's hope I'm wrong. Look, why don't you head home? I doubt we'll have many customers on a night like this, and I can close up. Besides, didn't you say Eileen wasn't feeling well? I'm sure you'd rather be home with her than holed up here with a grouchy bookseller."

Nancy smiled. "Well, if you're sure, I'll take you up on your offer. She just has a scratchy throat, but after that bout with strep last year I'm extra cautious. Mrs. Cook takes good care of her when I'm gone, but I'd feel better if I could check on her myself."

"Go. And be careful. It's a downpour."

Forty-five minutes later, as he worked on payroll in the back office, he heard the front door open. He glanced at his watch. Quarter to eight. It was either a last-minute customer or his tardy new partner. And he had a feeling he knew which it was. His lips settled into a grim line as he quickly logged off the computer and headed out front.

Blake had no idea what to expect when he stepped into the main room, but the dripping mess that greeted him wasn't it.

A woman stood just inside the entrance as a puddle rapidly formed at her feet on the gleaming hardwood floor. Her wet, strawberry blond hair straggled out of a lopsided topknot, and damp ringlets were stuck to her forehead. He couldn't quite decide what she was wearing—some sort of long-sleeved, hip-length tunic over what might once have been wide-legged trousers. Right now, the whole outfit was plastered to her willowy frame like a second, wrinkled skin.

She doesn't even know enough to come in out of the rain. The thought came to Blake unbidden, and he shook his head.

The slight movement caught A.J.'s eye, and she glanced over at the tall man who was looking at her with a mixture of disgust and resignation. Was this Blake Sullivan? If so, he sure didn't match the image she'd created in her mind. She'd envisioned a bookish type, fiftyish, probably wearing glasses, possibly balding, maybe a little round-shouldered, sporting a paunch. A fussy, precise and stern curmudgeon.

Well, the latter qualities might prove to be true of the man standing across from her. But she'd been dead wrong on the physical description. Blake Sullivan was tall—she classified anyone who topped her five-foot-ten frame as tall—with dark brown hair and intense, cobalt-colored eyes. His crisp, blue oxford shirt, beige slacks and well-polished leather shoes bordered on being preppy, though the effect was softened by rolled-up sleeves. His attire also showed off his athletic build—broad chest, lean hips, flat abdomen. And his shoulders were definitely not rounded.

A.J. tried not to flinch under his scrutiny. She could only imagine how she appeared. No, on second thought, she didn't even want to go there. She could read enough from the look in his eyes. So much for first impressions.

With more bravado than she felt, she straightened her shoulders, tilted up her chin and gazed directly at the man across from her. "I'm looking for Blake Sullivan."

He waited a moment, as if trying to decide whether he wanted to have anything to do with the pitiful vision in front of him or simply turn around and run. Finally, with obvious reluctance, he approached her, stopping a couple of feet away to fold his arms across his chest. "You've found him."

She swallowed and extended her hand. "I'm A. J. Williams."

Short of ignoring her courteous gesture, Blake had no choice but to narrow the gap between them so he could take her hand.

At closer range, he realized that A.J. was tall. She was probably a couple of inches shorter than him, but whatever shoes she had on put them almost eye-to-eye. If she'd been wearing any makeup prior to her dash through the storm, the rain had efficiently dispensed with it, giving her a fresh, natural look that actually had a certain appeal. There was a light dusting of freckles across her small, slightly turned-up nose, and thick lashes fringed deep green eyes highlighted with gold flecks. His gaze dropped to her lips, and lingered there a moment too long before he reached for her extended hand.

Given her height, he was surprised to discover that her hand felt small and delicate in his. But her grip was firm. At least it was until he felt a tremor run through it—and then throughout her body. He frowned.

"Are you okay?"

"A little ch-chilled. I'll be okay once I ch-change out

of these wet clothes." She withdrew her hand from his self-consciously.

"Don't you have an umbrella?"

"Of course. Somewhere in the U-Haul. Along with my coat. It was sunny and warm when I left Chicago. It generally gets nicer when you head south. But obviously not today. Then I had to park down the block because all the spots in front of the shop were taken. Which is why I'm sporting the drowned-rat look."

Blake pointedly glanced at his watch. "It was quite a bit warmer here earlier. When you were supposed to arrive."

A.J. flushed. "I'm sorry about that. But I didn't plan on running into major road construction. Or having a flat tire. I'm a little out of practice, so it took me a while to change it."

And she'd paid a price for doing so. Even before the blowout her hip had already begun to throb from her long hours confined behind the wheel. Dealing with the tire had only intensified her discomfort. She shifted from one foot to the other, trying in vain to alleviate the ache that she knew only a hot bath would soothe.

"You could have called," Blake responded.

"Not without a phone."

He looked surprised. "You don't have a cell phone?"

"No." Her budget barely allowed for a regular phone.

"It might be a good idea to get one...for emergencies."

She felt her temper begin to simmer at his condescending attitude, but she wasn't in a fighting mood tonight. Better to save her strength for the battles that she was beginning to suspect would surely follow in the days and weeks ahead. So, with an effort, she moderated her comments. "I'll consider that. But I'd hardly classify today as an emergency. And I already apologized for being late." Another shiver suddenly ran through her, and this time she made no attempt to hide it. "Look, can we continue this discussion on Monday? I came directly here and I'm cold and wet and hungry."

Blake had to admit that she did look pretty miserable. The puddle at her feet had widened, and there was definitely a chill in the shop. The heating system in the older building hadn't quite caught up with the sudden, late-afternoon plunge in temperature. So if *he* noticed the coolness in the air, she must be freezing.

"Monday is fine. Shall we say nine a.m.? That gives us an hour before the store opens."

"Fine."

He stuck out his hand. "Until Monday, then."

She seemed surprised by his gesture, but responded automatically. And his assessment was confirmed. Her fingers were like ice. He frowned, good manners warring with aggravation at her tardiness.

"Look, can I offer you a cup of tea first? We keep some on hand for the patrons."

Again, surprise flickered in her eyes—followed quickly by wariness. He supposed he couldn't blame her. He hadn't exactly been welcoming—or hospitable—up till now.

"Thanks. But I think a hot bath is the only thing that will chase the chill away."

His gaze scanned her slender form, and she suddenly realized her once loose-fitting outfit had become plastered to her skin. Her face flushed a deep red, and with her free hand she tried to pry the fabric away. When that attempt was unsuccessful, she tugged her other hand from Blake's and took a step back. "I'll see you Monday at nine." Her voice sounded a bit breathless.

"Do you have somewhere to stay tonight?"

"Yes. And a real estate agent lined up tomorrow to look at apartments."

He nodded. "Can I loan you an umbrella? It's still pouring."

She backed toward the door. "There's not much point now, is there?"

He glanced at the puddle on the floor in the spot she had just vacated. "True."

The crimson of her face went a shade deeper and her step faltered. "Oh…I'm sorry about that. I can clean it up, if you have a mop or…"

"Ms. Williams," Blake cut her off, but his tone was cordial. "I'll take care of this. Why don't you follow your own advice? Take a hot bath and have a hot meal. We'll make a fresh start on Monday. Okay?"

A.J. studied him for a moment. Did she detect a softening in his manner, a slight warmth in his tone? Or was it resignation? Or perhaps pity, because she was cold and wet and hungry and had a trying trip to St. Louis? Or was it pity for himself, because he'd been saddled with a partner who would need to be guided every step of the way?

If he thought the latter, he was in for a big surprise

come Monday. But for now, she *was* cold, wet and hungry—and definitely not at her best. So she needed to exit. As gracefully as possible.

With a curt nod, she turned toward the door. And tried not to run.

Chapter Two

At precisely nine o'clock Monday morning, A.J. knocked on the door at Turning Leaves. It was a gloriously sunny Indian summer day in mid-November, and as she waited for Blake to let her in, she surveyed the scene with a smile. Though Maplewood was a close-in suburb of St. Louis, this section had a small-town feel. The tree-lined streets and mom-and-pop shops hearkened back to another era, and morning walkers were already putting in their paces.

The door rattled, then swung inward as she turned back toward the shop. Blake stood on the other side, his clothes similar to what he'd worn on Friday except that he'd exchanged his blue oxford shirt for a yellow one, and his sleeves weren't yet rolled up. His hair was damp, as if he'd showered very recently.

"Good morning." She glanced at her watch. "You said nine o'clock, right?"

Blake ignored her question. If she expected him to

compliment her punctuality, she would be sorely disappointed. It was the least he expected. Besides, he was still trying to reconcile the woman standing across from him now with the bedraggled waif who had dripped water all over his floor Friday night. Her hair was lighter in color than he remembered, and her top-knot of natural curls was firmly in place. A few rebellious tendrils had fought their way out of the confining band to softly frame her face, which still seemed to be mostly makeup free. A touch of lipstick, perhaps some mascara, maybe a hint of blush—though the color in her cheeks could well be natural, he concluded. The sparkle in her eyes certainly was, enhanced by her open, friendly smile. It suddenly struck him that A. J. Williams was an extremely attractive woman. Not that he cared, of course.

When he didn't respond to her greeting, she turned again and made a sweeping gesture. "Isn't it a glorious day?"

Blake glanced around the familiar landscape. He'd jogged his usual eight miles before coming to work, but in all honesty he hadn't paid much attention to his surroundings. He'd been thinking about his training schedule for the upcoming triathlon, a late order that he needed to follow up on at the shop, invoices that needed to be reconciled…and a myriad of other things.

"Just look how blue the sky is," A.J. enthused. "And the sun feels so warm for November! I guess you haven't had a hard freeze yet, because the geraniums and petunias still look great."

Blake looked at the sky, then glanced at the flowers

in the planters along the street. He wouldn't have noticed either if A.J. hadn't pointed them out. And for some reason her comment made him feel as if he should have. Which aggravated him. He didn't need any guilt trips. What he needed was time to brief his new partner before the shop opened.

"If you're ready to come in, we can get started," he said shortly.

A.J. turned back to him and tilted her head. "No time to smell the flowers along the way, Mr. Sullivan?"

"I have work to do." His voice sounded unnaturally stiff even to his own ears.

"I think God would appreciate it if we took a moment to admire His handiwork, don't you?"

"I'm sure God has better things to think about. If He cares at all."

A.J. raised one eyebrow. "Do I detect a note of cynicism in that comment?"

Blake shrugged. "Whatever. Let's just say I haven't seen much evidence that God cares."

A.J.'s eyes grew sympathetic. "That's too bad. Because He does."

Blake frowned impatiently. "Look, can we just get down to business? Because we've only got an hour before the shop opens, and I'd like to show you around before the customers start coming."

"Absolutely. I'm ready whenever you are."

He stepped aside, and as she swept past he caught a faint, pleasing fragrance. Not floral. Not exotic. Just… fresh. It seemed to linger even after she moved away.

A.J. took a moment to look over the shop, something

she hadn't done Friday night. As she completed her circuit, her gaze returned to Blake. He was still at the door, and he was staring at her. She couldn't quite read the expression in his eyes, but it looked as if he'd found something else to disapprove of. Her chin lifted a notch.

"Anything wrong?" She tried to keep her tone mild, but a note of defiance crept in.

Blake studied her attire. She wore a white peasant-type blouse in some wrinkly fabric, and a funky bronze cross hung from a chain around her neck. An unusual metal belt cinched her impossibly small waist. Her skirt, made of several progressively longer layers of what appeared to be a patchwork of fabrics, brushed her legs mid-calf. If his attire bordered on preppy, hers could well be described as hippie. Which did not evoke happy memories.

"Mr. Sullivan, is something wrong?" she repeated more pointedly.

He frowned. "I haven't seen clothes like that in a long time."

She looked down and smoothed her skirt over her hips. "Probably not. They're from a vintage clothing store I discovered in Chicago. Pretty cool, huh?"

Actually, he had another word for her attire. But he settled for a less judgmental term. "Interesting."

The look she gave him told him very clearly that she knew exactly what his opinion was. And that, in turn, she had judged him to be stuffy, uptight and conventional. "Very diplomatic. I wasn't sure you had it in you." Before he could respond, she turned back to the shop. "So, how about that tour?"

Blake thought about responding to her comment—

then thought better of it. He had to work with this woman for the next six months, and it would be to both their advantages if they made an effort to get along.

"Sure. Let's start with a walk-through."

The shop wasn't huge, and A.J. only made a few comments as Blake showed her around. There was a small area for children's books, and sections devoted to books on travel, cooking, fiction, gardening and general nonfiction. There was also a reading nook, with four comfortable chairs, and a coffee and tea maker tucked in a back corner. A small stockroom and tidy office were behind a door marked "private." Two big picture windows flanked the front door, and each featured displays of the latest releases. The older building was well-maintained, with a high ceiling and hardwood floors, and A.J. felt comfortable in the space immediately. Just as she'd felt comfortable in the tiny apartment she'd found Saturday. It, too, was in an older building, in a neighborhood that had obviously seen better days. But it was safe and in the early stages of renewal, the real estate agent had assured her.

When the tour was over, Blake waited for her to say something.

"This is a great space," she said, choosing her words carefully. "It's sunny and bright and inviting. There's a nice selection of books. And the layout is…interesting."

She'd borrowed the word he'd used earlier to describe her attire, and Blake gave her a suspicious look. "What does that mean?"

She lifted one shoulder. "We might want to think about rearranging a few things."

He frowned. "Our customers seem to like this setup. We do quite well."

"Yes, that's what Seth Mitchell said. Which reminds me, I'd like to spend some time going over the accounts with you."

A flicker of amusement crept into his eyes. "That could be a little tedious. It might be better if I meet with your accountant. Or, if you don't have one, I'm sure Mr. Mitchell can recommend someone. But I'll be happy to answer any questions you might have today."

The condescending tone was back, but this time A.J. was ready for him. "That's kind of you," she said sweetly. "I do have a few."

"Shoot," he said amiably.

"Okay. Let's start with some basics. I'd like to get the details on return on capital, net profit, blue-sky value, inventory turnover rates, payroll expenses and any major debt. I'd also like to get some breakdowns on customer demographics, sales by book category, store traffic patterns and volume, and repeat customers. That's just to start, of course."

The dazed look on Blake's face was totally satisfying. As was the lengthy time it took for him to recover from her barrage of questions.

"I'm not sure I have all those answers at my fingertips," he said slowly. "It might take me a couple of days to pull the data together."

"Okay. I jotted down some other questions, too." She fished in her purse and withdrew two pages of additional typed questions and handed them to him. "You might as well work on these at the same time."

He scanned the list quickly, frowning, and when he looked back at her she could read the question in his eyes. She answered it before he could ask.

"I have an M.B.A. From Wharton. I chose not to pursue a business career for a variety of reasons. But I have the background. And it's kind of like riding a bicycle. You never forget."

Blake felt his neck grow warm. Jo had long ago taught him not to judge a book by its cover. Yet that was exactly what he'd done with A.J. She didn't look like a businesswoman. At least not his image of one. So he'd assumed she had no business skills. He felt suitably chastised—but he didn't like being made a fool of. "Why didn't you tell me?"

She shrugged. "You seemed to have your mind made up about me from our first conversation. So I figured I'd wait and play my hand when the time was right. Which turned out to be today."

So A.J. *wasn't* some ditzy airhead after all, he conceded. She had business savvy. Quite a bit of it, if the questions she was asking were any indication. But it was only textbook knowledge. She might be able to analyze the balance sheet, but she had no practical experience. And he did. He knew the book business. So she needed him. Which meant he still had some leverage. And some control. That knowledge gave him some comfort. Because ever since Jo's death and A.J.'s first phone call, he'd been watching his control erode. And it was not a good feeling.

When the silence lengthened, A.J. sighed. "Look, I'm sorry if you jumped to conclusions about me. Obviously, I have the financial background to run this shop. But I don't have practical experience. I guess Aunt Jo hoped you'd teach me. And I'm willing to learn. So can we just start over? Otherwise it's going to be a long six months."

Blake couldn't argue with that. "Maybe it would help if we set some ground rules."

She made a face. "Why don't we just take it a day at a time? Make up the rules as we go along?"

"You mean wing it?"

"More or less."

"That's not the best way to run a business." Or a life, as far as he was concerned. He liked rules and structure. He'd had enough of "winging it" to last a lifetime.

"We're not a Fortune 500 company, Blake. We can afford to be a little flexible."

That was another word he hated. Too often "flexible" became an excuse for not honoring commitments.

At his grim expression, A.J. grinned. "Loosen up, Blake. Life's too short to sweat the small stuff."

"I don't consider Turning Leaves small stuff," he said stiffly, sounding uncharacteristically pompous and self-righteous even to his own ears. This woman just brought out the worst in him.

"I didn't say it was. I was referring to your ground rules. I don't want to get hung up on making a lot of guidelines that may not be necessary. Let's just work things out as we go along. And before you know it, the six months will zip right by."

The bell jangled over the door, and A.J. turned her

attention to the customer who had just entered. "Oh, look at that darling little girl!"

Blake glanced at the young mother and her child. The toddler looked to be about four, and she was clutching a glazed donut. Which translated to sticky fingers—and sticky merchandise. He started forward, then stopped. The house rules said no food in the shop. But he had a feeling the house rules were about to go out the window.

Blake sighed. It was going to be a long six months.

"I'd like to start closing the shop on Sundays."

Blake stared at A.J. as if she'd lost her mind. Their first week as partners had been remarkably smooth. She was an eager learner, and Blake was beginning to think that maybe this arrangement would work out after all. Until she'd dropped this bombshell.

"Excuse me?"

She looked up from the catalog of new releases she was perusing. "I'd like to close the shop on Sundays."

"Why? We're always busy on Sunday."

"I've studied the traffic and sales data. We do have a lot of window-shoppers on Sunday. But it's not one of our bigger sales days. And we're only open for five hours, anyway. I don't think we'll notice much impact on our bottom line."

This was exactly the kind of impetuous action that Blake had been afraid of. Out of the corner of his eye he caught Nancy observing the exchange, and he took a deep breath before responding.

"I don't think changing the hours is a good idea.

Everyone else on the street is open on Sunday. Our customers will be disappointed."

"We can change our phone message and have a sign with our new hours made for the window. People will adjust."

He raked his fingers through his hair. "Why is this such a big deal? Sunday hours are convenient for our customers and we always have enough sales to justify being open."

A.J. closed the catalog and looked at him steadily. "My main reason for wanting to close has nothing to do with sales or with customers. Sunday is the Lord's day. A day of rest. A day to keep holy. A store like ours that sells nonessential items doesn't need to be open."

Blake stared at her. "You're kidding."

Her gaze didn't waver. "Do I look like I'm kidding?"

He tried a different approach. "Jo was very religious. And *she* was open on Sunday."

"When did she start opening on Sunday?"

"A couple of years ago."

About the time he took over the day-to-day management of the shop. Neither voiced that thought, but it hung in the air.

"Did she work in the shop that day?" A.J. asked.

"No."

"Who did?"

"Nancy and I alternated."

A.J. glanced over at Nancy. She didn't know the part-time worker very well yet, but she'd learned enough to know that the divorced mother had a tough life, that she juggled two part-time jobs just to make ends meet, and that she was a churchgoing woman with a quiet, deep faith.

"How do you feel about it, Nancy?" A.J. asked.

Nancy looked uncertainly from A.J. to Blake, then back again. "I need the job, A.J. I'll be happy to work whatever hours you and Blake give me."

A.J. smiled. "I already know that, Nancy. That's not what I'm asking. How do you feel about working on Sundays?"

"Well, the money is nice." She hesitated. "But it's always a rush to get here after church, and then I have to leave Eileen with Mrs. Cook all afternoon. I guess, if I had a choice, I'd prefer to have Sundays off so I could spend a little more time at church and with my daughter. Six days of work ought to be enough for anyone. Even God rested on the seventh day."

Blake stared at Nancy. "You never said anything to me about not wanting to work on Sundays."

"I didn't think it was an option."

He expelled a frustrated breath. "Okay, fine. I don't mind working. We can surely find someone to fill in every other weekend for those few hours."

"I'm sure we can, Blake," A.J. replied calmly. "But that's not the point. I'm talking about principles here. And if you're worried about losing sales, I'm sure we can find a way to make up the difference."

"Such as?"

"I'm working on it."

He looked at her, and the determination in her eyes told him that she was dead set on this. He didn't agree, but he wasn't sure it was worth waging a major battle over. Yes, they'd lose some sales. But she was right. The decision wouldn't make or break the shop. Besides, he suspected there would be bigger battles to fight down the road. Maybe the best strategy was to let her win this one.

"Okay. If that's what you want. I just hope you don't regret it," he capitulated.

"I don't waste my time on regrets, Blake. They're all about the past. I try to focus on today and make the best decisions I can."

"Well, it wouldn't hurt to think a little bit about tomorrow, too."

A shadow crossed her eyes, so fleeting that he thought perhaps it was just the play of light as she turned her head. "Tomorrow has a way of surprising us, no matter what we plan," she said quietly.

Blake didn't know what to make of that comment. So he simply turned away and headed back to the office.

Nancy watched him go, then moved to the counter beside A.J. "I applaud your position."

A.J. turned to her with a rueful smile. "I'm glad someone does."

"Don't mind Blake. It's been a hard transition for him. He and Jo went way back, and he took her death pretty hard. Plus, he's more or less run the shop for the past couple of years, so having a partner is a big adjustment for him. But he's a great guy when you get to know him. He's really conscientious, and you won't ever meet a kinder, more considerate person. He even came over to my apartment one night last winter at three in the morning when I was worried about Eileen, and then drove us to the emergency room."

A.J. frowned. Were they talking about the same Blake? She didn't doubt the conscientious part, but kind and considerate? She hadn't seen much evidence of those qualities.

When A.J. didn't immediately respond, Nancy smiled knowingly. "You'll find out after you get to know him. But what I really wanted to ask was if you'd like to join me for church on Sunday. After your comments about closing, I figured you must be in the habit of attending church, and since you're new in town I wasn't sure if you'd had a chance yet to find a place to worship. We have a great congregation, and our minister is wonderful. You'd be welcomed warmly."

In fact, A.J. was in the habit of weekly worship, but so far she'd been too busy settling in to have a chance to seek out a new church. Nancy's invitation was perfectly timed. "Thank you. That would be great."

Blake came out from the office, but on his way back to the front counter, he was waylaid by a customer. Nancy glanced his way.

"I've invited Blake a few times, too, but so far I haven't had any luck," she offered, lowering her voice.

A.J. thought about his comments to her when she'd mentioned God. "He doesn't strike me as a religious man."

"I think he believes in God. But he wasn't raised in a religious environment. It's hard to convince someone who is so self-reliant that the plans we make for our life don't always match God's. Blake's kind of a loner, and he's so used to relying only on himself that I just don't think he's willing to put his life in anyone else's hands. Even God's."

A.J. looked over at the tall, dark-haired man deep in conversation with a customer. He was angled slightly away from her, and she had a good view of his profile—strong chin, well-shaped nose, nicely formed lips. Self-reliance was a good thing in moderation. A.J. knew that from personal experience. But she couldn't imagine taking it to such an extreme that she shut other people out of her life. Especially God. It would be a very empty existence.

Suddenly Blake glanced at her, almost as if he knew she was watching him. Their gazes met, and whatever he saw in hers—curiosity, sympathy, or a combination of both—brought a frown to his face. She responded with a smile. And even though he didn't physically move, she felt almost as if he'd taken a step back. And posted a sign saying Private. No Trespassing.

A.J. didn't really care if he kept his distance. Their relationship was destined to be short-lived, anyway. But she wasn't used to having her gestures of friendship so openly rebuffed. She turned back to find Nancy watching the exchange.

"Blake doesn't let too many people get close," Nancy noted. "Even I don't know much about his background, and we've worked together for almost two years."

A.J. shrugged. "I respect people's privacy. If he wants to shut people out, it doesn't matter to me."

But as she headed to the back room to check the new

inventory, she realized that her answer hadn't been quite honest. Because in that brief, unguarded moment, before his barriers had slipped back into place, she'd glimpsed in Blake's eyes a stark loneliness that had touched her deep inside.

And even though they were practically strangers, even though he clearly resented her presence at Turning Leaves, even though he disapproved of almost everything she did, that loneliness troubled her. More than she cared to admit.

And she had no idea why.

"So…what do you think?"

Blake had only been gone from the shop for four days. Just a quick trip to Cincinnati to compete in a triathlon over Thanksgiving weekend. But if he'd been gone three weeks, the shop couldn't have changed more dramatically.

He stood rooted just inside the door of the office, trying to absorb the changes that had been wrought in his absence. Gone was the table of featured books and the greeting card rack that had been just inside the display window on the left. Now the four chairs from the reading nook were arranged there, and a low, square table that he didn't recognize was placed in front of them, with a small pot of copper-colored chrysanthemums in the center. Two chairs were on one side of the table, facing the window, with the others at right angles on the adjacent two sides. A couple of the chairs were occupied, and one of the patrons was helping himself to a cup of coffee from the coffee and tea maker that had also been moved to the front of the shop. Blake recognized him as a regular, though not someone who usually bought much.

"Well?" A.J. prompted.

Slowly, Blake turned to his partner. Her eyes were sparkling with excitement, but he could also sense some trepidation. She knew him well enough even after only a couple of weeks to realize that he didn't like sudden, unplanned changes.

"What happened to the display table? And the cards?"

"The table's in the back room. I moved the cards closer to the checkout counter." She gestured over her shoulder.

He planted his fists on his hips and studied the new arrangement. It was attractive enough. But it changed the dynamics of the shop entirely. And it definitely cut down on display space.

"What did you do with the old reading nook?"

"Come see."

She led him to the back corner, which had been transformed into a small enclosure complete with blocks, vinyl books and an assortment of toys. He frowned and looked at her questioningly. "What's this?"

"A play area. A lot of people come in here with toddlers and young children, and it's pretty difficult to look through books when you're juggling a little one. Now they can safely leave their children here to play while they make their selections."

He grunted in response.

"Several mothers have already commented on how much they like this." There was a slight defensive note in her voice.

"And what about the area in front? You've lost a lot of display space. That sells books."

"So does atmosphere. When people walk by and see patrons relaxing and enjoying themselves through the window, they might be more inclined to come in and look around. Besides, the other reading nook wasn't being used much. The light wasn't very good, and it was so tucked away a lot of people missed it. But it makes a perfect play spot."

Before he could respond, the bell on the front counter rang. The regular patron Blake had noticed in the new sitting area was waiting to purchase a large coffee-table book.

"Morning, folks," he said cheerily as they joined him.

"Good morning." A.J. reached for the book and started to ring up the sale while Blake retrieved a bag from under the counter.

The older man took a sip of his coffee. "By the way, my compliments on the new reading area. Never did like that one stuck back in the corner. Not enough light for these old eyes. This one is real cheerful and bright."

Out of the corner of his eye, Blake saw A.J. give him a sidelong glance, but he kept his gaze averted. "Thank you. We hope you'll come back soon."

"You can count on it. Thanks again."

They watched as the man exited, the bell jangling as the door closed behind him. Blake knew A.J. was looking at him. Waiting for him to compliment her on what she'd done, especially in light of the customer's unsolicited approval. But he didn't want to encourage her. Change was fine, as long as it was planned. And carefully thought out. And discussed. But he had a real issue with spur-of-the-moment changes. Because in his experience, most of the time they weren't good ones.

"I saw some new inventory in the back when I got here. I'll log it in," he said.

He turned to go, but her voice stopped him. "Did you have a nice Thanksgiving?"

. He'd been expecting a comment on the new layout, so it took him a moment to switch gears…and formulate an answer. He'd spent most of Thanksgiving Day training for the triathlon, then he'd eaten a frozen turkey dinner at home. He'd been on the road early the next morning for Cincinnati, spent Saturday competing, then drove home Sunday. His parents had invited him to visit for the holiday, of course. They always did. And, as always, he'd refused. But A.J. didn't need to know any of that. "Yes," he replied briefly. "How about you?"

She smiled. "I had a great Thanksgiving. I don't know anyone here, so I joined a group from Nancy's church to help feed the homeless downtown. And we got a great turkey dinner in the bargain."

He frowned. Dishing up food for a bunch of down-and-out strangers didn't sound like a great holiday to him. It hit too close to home. His parents had never resorted to a homeless shelter, but they'd come close a few times. "Don't you have family?" Hadn't Jo mentioned several great-nieces? But he couldn't recall any details.

"My parents are both gone. But I have two sisters. They're too far away to visit for such a short holiday. We'll make up for it at Christmas, I hope." She'd talked to them both, of course. Morgan had actually gone to work in the morning, then out to dinner with friends. And Clare had somehow managed to wrangle a holiday dinner invitation to the same place Dr. Wright and his daughter were going. There was no stopping Clare when she set her mind to something, A.J. thought with a grin. "What about you, Blake? Any family?"

Slowly he shook his head. "No brothers or sisters. My parents live in Oregon."

"Also too far away for Thanksgiving. Maybe you can see them at Christmas."

Not likely, Blake thought. But she didn't need to know that. He started to turn away, but suddenly found himself speaking. "By the way, I like what you did with the shop."

A.J. looked as surprised by the comment as he was. He had no idea where those words had come from. He'd certainly had no intention of complimenting her. But she rewarded him with a dazzling smile. "Thank you."

Suddenly Blake felt as if he'd just hit the proverbial runner's wall. It was a familiar experience that squeezed the breath out of his lungs and left him feeling limp when it occurred at about the twenty-one mile mark of a marathon.

But the only thing racing right now was his heart.

Which made no sense.

And it made him want to run as fast as he could away from this red-haired source of disruption in his life.

Chapter Three

"I think I figured out a way to make up the Sunday sales."

Blake's stomach clenched. Barely a week had passed since A.J. had rearranged the shop, and now she was on to something else. Which meant more upheaval. Change seemed to be this woman's middle name. Warily he looked up from the computer screen.

A.J. shifted a large box in her arms and smiled. "Chill out, Blake. Maybe you'll like my idea."

He doubted it, and his skeptical expression told her so.

"Maybe not," she amended. "But here it is anyway." She placed the box on a chair and began pulling out a variety of items, which she lined up on the desk. "It occurred to me that people who are shopping for books are often shopping for gifts. Now, there are plenty of gift shops around. But not many that carry items like these, handmade in third-world countries. Good Samaritan, where I used to work, is starting a craft program, and a portion of the profits from the sales will benefit the artists. A lot of people in those countries are in desperate need of income, and a program like this is a godsend for them. Plus, I think it will drive traffic to our shop and more than make up for any sales we've lost by closing on Sunday. It's a win-win situation all around, don't you think?"

Blake looked at the array of items now displayed on his desk. Wood carvings, metalwork, woven placemats, pottery. Some were crude folk art. Others reflected great skill and artistry. None seemed appropriate for the bookshop. Nor was there room to display them without sacrificing space for their primary product.

A.J. spoke before he could offer his opinion. "Lots of bookstores carry small gift items," she pointed out. "And space isn't really a problem. I thought we'd intersperse a few items in the display window among the books. They'll add some visual interest. And I found out the jewelry store next door is getting new display cases. I asked Steve about buying one of his old ones to replace our sales counter, and when he found out what I was going to use it for, he offered to donate it. So we'll be able to display a lot of these items without taking any space away from the books. Isn't that great?"

Blake stared at A.J. After three years, he knew Steve Winchell, the owner of the jewelry store, well enough to say hello when they met in the parking lot. But that was about it. In less than a month, A.J. was on a first name basis with all of their neighbors.

"Earth to Blake."

He caught her teasing tone and frowned. "This might dilute book sales."

"I don't think so. In fact, I think these items will draw new customers into the shop, and they might end up buying books as well. Plus, I bet some of our regular book customers will also buy these items as gifts. We can monitor it, though. If I'm wrong, I'm certainly willing to reconsider."

But she wasn't wrong. Within the first week, that was obvious. Blake told himself that part of the success of the new merchandise was due to the approaching holidays. It was just a gift-buying season. He suspected sales would taper off after Christmas. But even if they did, even if they only generated a modest return, it was all incremental. Because, thanks to A.J.'s creativity, the new offerings hadn't taken one iota of space away from books. Exchanging their old checkout counter for the display case had been an ingenious solution. But Blake hadn't told A.J. that. She didn't need encouragement. And he didn't need more disruptions.

But he had a feeling they were coming, anyway.

"Blake, could I speak with you when you have a minute?"

He looked toward A.J. while he waited for a customer to sign a credit card slip. She stood in the door of the office, and there was something in her eyes that made his stomach clench.

Here we go again, he thought, steeling himself for whatever brainstorm A.J. had just had.

"Sure. I'll be right with you." He finished the sale,

then glanced toward the young woman restocking the cookbook section. "Trish, can you watch the front desk for a few minutes?"

"Sure, Mr. Sullivan." The perky teen who helped out a few days a week after school made her way over to the counter. She smiled brightly. "Take your time."

She'd love that, Blake thought. Trish wasn't the hardest worker they'd ever had. But front desk duty suited her to a T. She was sweet and friendly, which counted for something, he supposed.

When he entered the office, A.J. was studying a recent order, a frown marring her usually smooth brow. She looked up when he walked in.

"What's up?" he asked, willing himself to remain cool.

"I'd like to cancel a couple of the selections we've ordered."

Now it was his turn to frown. "Which ones?" When she named them, his frown deepened. "Those are sure to be bestsellers. Our customers will expect us to stock them."

"Have you read the ARCs?"

"No." He rarely had time to read the advance copies sent out by publishers.

"I took them home over the weekend. I didn't read them thoroughly, but skimmed through enough to know trash when I see it."

"Those authors are extremely popular. A lot of people must not agree with you."

"A lot of people read trash."

He folded his arms across his chest and struggled to

keep his temper in check. "So you're trying to impose your values on everyone else."

She'd wrestled with that very dilemma all weekend. How to reconcile personal values with bottom-line business decisions. It was the same conflict she'd grappled with in graduate school. And had worried about facing in the business world when she graduated. As it turned out, she'd never had to deal with it. Until now.

Blake sensed her uncertainty and pressed his advantage. "It sounds a little like censorship to me."

A.J. sighed and distractedly brushed some wayward tendrils off her forehead. "I know. But I've given it a lot of thought. I don't see how, in good conscience, we can carry books that are so blatantly sensational. I'm fine with books that deal with gritty themes or realistically portray bad situations, but in these novels all of the gore and sex and violence is just for effect. There's absolutely no redeeming social value."

"In *your* opinion."

"And God's. I talked with my pastor about this. I think this is the right thing to do, Blake. Our shop isn't that big. We can't carry every book. So I think we should focus on carrying *good* books."

Blake didn't agree with her position. But he couldn't help admiring her. She had principles. And she didn't compromise them. That was a rare trait in today's world. Jo had been like that, too. And so were his parents, he admitted grudgingly. Maybe he didn't like their principles, either. But they'd stuck with them.

"We're going to have some unhappy customers," he pointed out.

"I realize that. We'll just have to explain our position and hope they understand."

"*Our* position?"

"Okay, *my* position."

"We'll also lose sales. People who want those books will go somewhere else. There's an impact on the bottom line here."

"I know. And I realize that affects both of us, since we each own half of the business. But I feel very strongly about this, Blake. So I'd at least like to give it a try. If we take a huge hit, I'm willing to discuss it again and consider other alternatives. But I'd like to try it for a month or two. Can you live with that?"

He folded his arms across his chest. "We won't get back the customers we lose."

"Maybe we'll pick up some new ones."

Blake supposed he could fight A.J. on this. But she had taken his concerns into consideration and was willing to discuss it if things didn't work out. He supposed he could at least give her the time she had requested to test the waters. "Okay. Let's try it for a few weeks. You don't mind if I funnel any questions about this your way, do you?"

"No. It was my decision. I'll defend it."

And that's exactly what she had to do a few days later when a customer asked Blake about one of the books A.J. had canceled. A.J. overheard the question and, true to her word, quickly stepped in. She glanced down at the signature line on the credit card slip the woman had just signed.

"Mrs. Renner, I'm A. J. Williams, one of the owners of Turning Leaves. I wanted to let you know that we're not going to be carrying that title. As you can see, we're a small shop, so we have to be very selective of our inventory. Quite honestly, not all bestselling books have content that's worthy of our limited space. I've reviewed an advance copy of that book, and I'm afraid it just didn't make the cut."

The woman looked surprised. "That sounds like the philosophy at the Christian bookstore I go to. I didn't realize secular bookstores were so diligent."

"I don't think most are. But we're small enough that we can be a little more careful."

"Well, that's good to know. I have to admit, some of the novels I've read have shocked me. But you never know until you've already bought the book. It's nice to think that a secular store has some standards, too."

Not all patrons were so understanding, of course. But Blake had to admit that A.J. handled all the comments—and complaints—with grace and honesty.

Blake doubted that he and A.J. would ever see eye-to-eye on how to run the business. But, by and large, her decisions had been good ones. He glanced toward the reading nook. In its former location, it was rare for more than one chair to be occupied. Now patrons vied for the seats. Since they'd added the play area for children, young mothers and grandparents lingered longer in the shop. And they'd had to restock the glass display case regularly to keep up with the demand for the craft items, which had more than compensated for the sales lost by closing on Sunday.

Blake still didn't think this latest decision would be

as good for business. But it was consistent. A.J. might be a go-with-the-flow kind of woman, but in one thing she was very predictable. She stuck to her convictions.

He glanced toward her as she helped a patron select a book on gardening. Her head was bent as she listened intently to the older woman, and the late-afternoon light from the window gave her skin a golden glow. He watched as she turned to scan the selection of garden books, a slight frown on her brow, her lithe form silhouetted by the light. A moment later she reached up to select a thin volume. He was struck once again by her slender, graceful hands, recalling the night she'd arrived and his surprise when he'd reached for her hand in greeting. Because of her height, he'd been taken aback by its delicacy. And maybe he was just getting used to her funky clothes, but he was suddenly able to look past her attire and recognize that A.J. was, in fact, a lovely woman.

With a will of iron.

"A.J., do you have a minute?"

A.J. turned to find George from the Greek restaurant down the block standing at the end of the aisle. He looked agitated, and she frowned. "Sure. What's up?"

"Can I speak with you, someplace private?"

"The office is about as private as it gets around here." She headed toward the front desk. "Trish, I'll be in the back with Mr. Pashos. Stay at the desk, okay? Blake should be back from lunch any minute."

"Sure thing." The girl happily climbed on a stool behind the counter and proceeded to inspect her nails.

A.J. led the way toward the office, and motioned George to a seat. "Is everything okay?"

He sat, but leaned forward intently and shook his head. "Nothing is okay. Do you know about this thing called TIF?"

"No. What is it?"

"It stands for tax increment financing. The government can use it to help develop areas where—how do you say?—the economic potential isn't being maximized."

A.J. frowned. "Okay. So why is this upsetting you?"

George stood and began to pace. "There is a developer who wants to buy this block and put in a retail and residential development. He has already started the process."

Twin furrows appeared on A.J.'s brow. "But what if we don't want to sell?"

"That is where TIF comes in. If he can convince the city that his development will generate more revenue for Maplewood, we could all be shut down."

"But that's wrong!"

"Of course it is wrong! Your aunt, she would fight this! She was the first one to open a shop here, more than twenty years ago, when this area was not so good and businesses were closing, not opening. She believed in this area. And she persuaded others to follow. Your aunt, she was good at that. After we became friends and she found out that Sophia and I wanted to start our own restaurant, she helped us. We would not have our restaurant if it was not for her generosity and kindness, may the Lord be with her. And then others followed. Joe at the bakery, and Alene at the natural food store. Rose at the deli has been here for many years, and so has Steve. Carlos at the art gallery is the newest, but he has been here for ten years, too. We were the pioneers. We took a chance and invested in this area. And now that it is hot and trendy, what do we get? They want to throw us out! It is not right! The whole character of the neighborhood, it will change!" George's accent grew thicker as he spoke, and his agitation increased.

"There must be a way to stop this," A.J. reasoned. "Have you talked to any of the others?"

"No, not yet. I come to you first. You and Jo, you seem the same in many ways. Kind and caring. I did not think you would want your aunt's legacy to be sacrificed just so more money could be made by a rich developer. I think maybe you might have an idea."

A.J. tapped a pencil against the desk, frowning thoughtfully. "Well, I certainly believe there's strength in numbers. I guess the first thing we need to do is tell all the merchants on this block what's going on, and then have a meeting. If we all put our heads together, I'm sure we can come up with something."

"A meeting. Yes, that is a good way to start. But soon, A.J. We cannot waste time."

"I agree. Why don't we see if everyone is available Thursday night? We can have the meeting here, after the shop closes."

"Good. I will check. And I will bring baklava. It is always good to eat when you are trying to think." He pumped A.J.'s hand. "I knew the day you came down to introduce yourself that you would be a good neighbor, just like your aunt. I tell that to Sophia when you left. Now I know even more that it is true. I talk to you soon."

A.J. watched George leave. His spirits seemed higher, now that they had a preliminary action plan. But A.J. wasn't feeling so upbeat. Fighting city hall was never easy, especially when money was involved. But she didn't want to lose Aunt Jo's legacy before she even claimed it. So if a battle was brewing, she was more than willing to do her part.

She was still sitting in the office a few minutes later when Blake walked in carrying a bag from the deli. He took one look at her face and came to an abrupt halt. "What's wrong?"

She sighed and propped her chin in her hand. "We have a problem."

Slowly, Blake set the bag down on the desk, eyeing her warily. "Does this have anything to do with more changes in the shop?"

"Possibly. But not of my making."

By the time she explained the situation, Blake was frowning, too. He pulled up a chair and sat across from her. "I don't like the sound of this."

"Neither do I. I told George we could have a meeting here Thursday, when the shop closes, to discuss our next step. He's going to let the other merchants on the block know. You've been here longer than I have. Do you think they'll be willing to close ranks and go to battle over this?"

Blake shrugged. "I don't know. I've never exchanged more than a few words with any of them."

A.J. looked at him in surprise. She'd made it a point within the first couple of weeks to visit each shop and introduce herself. Blake had been here three years and he still didn't know his neighbors?

A flush crept up Blake's neck. When he spoke, there was a defensive tone to his voice. "I don't have time to socialize when I'm at work."

"I didn't say anything," A.J. pointed out. "Well, I guess we'll find out how they feel at the meeting. In the meantime, I need to do some research on this whole TIF thing. We better have all our facts in order before we take on a fight like this."

"My next-door neighbor works at city hall. I can try to get some information from him, too," Blake volunteered—with obvious reluctance.

"That would be good." A.J. sat back in her chair and shook her head. "You know, when I came here I thought my biggest challenge would be learning the book business. I didn't expect to have to fight city hall for my legacy."

"Neither did I. And I have a feeling this could get pretty messy."

A.J. studied Blake. He didn't look any too thrilled with that idea. "I take it you prefer to stay out of messy fights?"

He shrugged stiffly. "I prefer to stay out of fights of any kind. It's a lot easier when people can settle their differences quietly."

"True. But that doesn't always happen. And some things are worth fighting for." When he didn't respond, she stood and moved toward the door, but paused on the threshold to turn toward him. "So do you plan to come to the meeting on Thursday?"

Although his expression told her that he'd prefer to be almost anywhere else, he slowly nodded. "Yeah. I'll be there. I'm no more eager to lose this shop than you are. But this isn't my kind of thing."

"I gathered that. Thank you for making the effort. Maybe we'll come up with a way to settle this problem quietly, like you prefer."

"Maybe." But he had a gut feeling that wasn't going to happen.

And he suspected A.J. did, too.

As the group began to gather on Thursday night, Blake stayed in the background, feeling out of place and awkward—unlike A.J., who was mingling effortlessly with the diverse group, he noted. In the short time she'd been at the shop, she was already on a first-name basis with all of her fellow merchants and seemed to know their life histories. A few minutes before, he'd overheard her asking Rose how her grandson was doing in graduate school. And now she was talking to Joe about his wife's recent surgery. She had a knack for making friends and putting people at ease, something Blake had never mastered. Probably because he'd never been in one place long enough when he was growing up to learn those social skills, he thought.

They'd supplemented the seating area in the reading nook with folding chairs, and now A.J. moved to the front of the makeshift meeting room. "Okay, everyone, let's get started. I know George and Sophia have to get back to the restaurant as soon as possible, and Carlos is getting ready for an opening at the gallery tomorrow. So we need to keep this as brief as possible. George has already filled all of you in on the background, so the meeting tonight is really just a discussion to see how everyone feels about this."

"I think it stinks." Everyone turned toward Alene, who ran the natural food store. "We've all been here for years. Long before this area was hot. We put our blood, sweat and tears into these businesses, and we didn't get any help from city hall. If it wasn't for people like us, this area would never have revived. I say we fight it."

"I agree," Steve concurred. "When I opened my jewelry store, I had a tough time getting insurance. And for years, my premiums were elevated because of the crime rate in this area. I almost left once. But Jo convinced me to stay. She said if we stuck it out, eventually people would rediscover this place. And she was right. I'm not about to let some developer with dollar signs in his eyes take advantage of the turnaround at my expense."

Joe stood. "But what can we do? There are only a few of us. And if this means more money for Maplewood, the city won't care about us. They'll brush us aside."

"Not if we get more people behind us," Rose spoke up. Despite her gray hair and frail appearance, her clear blue eyes were steely. "The kind of development George described will ruin the neighborhood feel of this area. I don't think the residents will like that. I've already been talking to people about this when they stop in for their morning coffee and bagels. I bet the residents will stand behind us."

"I think we need to find out more," George said. "Like, who is this developer? And what has he done so far?"

Blake cleared his throat, and A.J. glanced his way. "Blake?"

"I was able to get some information from a pretty good source that might answer a few questions," he said. Seven pairs of eyes turned in his direction. "The developer is MacKenzie Properties. They've done this sort of thing in a number of municipalities in the area. They're very quiet and very successful, and if there's been any opposition, it's been squelched at a pretty early stage. Stuart MacKenzie is the principal and has been the primary contact at this preliminary stage with the Maplewood city hall."

"So what does he have in mind?" Alene asked.

Blake turned toward her. "George's information about the development plans is correct. MacKenzie is looking at a combination residential and commercial development over this entire block that would consist of high-end condos, office space and small shops. In the past, he's managed to get a TIF ruling, which means that existing residents are paid a predetermined sum for their businesses. In some cases, space is available in the new development for current merchants, but generally at a substantially higher cost. I believe most of us currently own our space. Under the new scenario, we'd have to lease space."

"What's the timing, Blake?" A.J. asked.

He looked her way. She seemed impressed by the information he'd relayed, which he'd only managed to gather this evening when he'd gone home for an early dinner and finally caught up with his neighbor. There was something in her eyes—warmth, gratitude…something—that made him feel proud of the little he'd done. "This is still in the very preliminary stages. MacKenzie will be presenting proposals to the city in mid-January, and there will be a public hearing in early February. It's unlikely a final ruling will be made before March or April. And I'm told that public opinion will factor heavily into the decision."

"It sounds like our work is cut out for us," Steve said.

"We need petitions," Alene added. "And press coverage."

"My nephew works for Channel 2. I can call him," Joe offered.

"Let's start with the petitions," A.J. said. "We can develop a form and ask our customers to begin signing them when they visit our businesses. We have almost six weeks until the public hearing in February, so we should be able to gather a lot of signatures. And maybe we can enlist local customers to circulate petitions in their neighborhoods, too."

"I can draw a form up for everyone to review," Steve volunteered.

"Thanks. That would be great. Let's meet again in mid-January and see where we stand. Does that sound good?"

There was a rumble of agreement at A.J.'s suggestion.

"And now everyone must have some baklava," George said. "It is just made today."

As the shop owners moved toward the coffee and pastries, A.J. made her way over to Blake, who still hovered in the background. "Thanks for digging up that information."

"It wasn't hard."

"So are you going to have some baklava? Or do you avoid sweets, too?"

He frowned at her. "What do you mean, 'too'?"

She shrugged. "Well, you don't mingle much. I found out recently that Carlos didn't even know you."

"I'm not into contemporary art."

For a moment she looked as if she was going to say something more on the subject, then changed her mind. "I think it was a good meeting."

He nodded. "But there's a lot of work ahead."

"Everyone seems willing to pitch in, though. And I'm sure Aunt Jo would have been leading the charge if she was here."

Blake couldn't argue with that. Jo had felt passionate about the shop and the neighborhood. So did the other merchants. And like it or not, he was in as deeply as everyone else. He still didn't want to get into the middle of a fight, but he'd found out enough to know that's probably where they were headed unless they rolled over and played dead. And much as he disliked confrontation, he wasn't ready to do that.

Yet.

Chapter Four

"Hi, A.J. Did you have a good time in North Carolina over Christmas?"

A.J. turned toward Rose with a smile as she recalled her visit with Clare. "Yes. It was wonderful."

"Did your sister Morgan make it down?"

"Unfortunately, no. She couldn't get away from work for more than a couple of days, so she went to Aunt Jo's cottage in Maine instead. But we all talked by phone. How about you? Did that grandson of yours make it home?"

"He sure did. He's still here, in fact. Goes back next week." She held up a stack of papers. "I've got another batch of petitions."

"That's great! I'll add them to the pile."

"So how many signatures do we have so far?"

A.J. did a quick mental calculation. "About five hundred, I think."

"Not bad. And I've been sending the form home

with some of my patrons to circulate in their neighborhoods. Is our meeting still on for next Thursday?"

"Yes. Same time, same place."

"Well, I'll be here. I'm not going to let some fancy developer run me out of here." Rose looked over A.J.'s shoulder. "Hi, Blake."

"Hello, Rose." He came up beside A.J. and glanced at the sheaf of papers in her hand. "Looks like you've been busy."

"I figure it's gonna take a lot of work from all of us if we want to win this fight. Now I gotta get back to the deli. See you both Thursday."

They watched her leave, then A.J. turned to Blake with a grin. "I hope I have half her energy and spunk when I'm that age."

"Why do I think that won't be a problem?"

She tilted her head and looked at him warily. "I'm not quite sure how to take that remark."

A smile tugged at the corners of his mouth. "Let's just say you have energy and spunk to spare."

"Why do I think that's not necessarily a compliment?" she replied.

He shrugged. "There's never a dull moment when you're around, that's for sure."

She studied him. Considering that Blake liked things predictable and well-planned, she figured that his comment was not a compliment. Which bothered her for some reason. But she shrugged it off and turned toward the office, waving the petitions at him. "I'm going to file these with the rest. Watch the desk, okay?" Without waiting for a response, she disappeared into the back room.

Blake watched her go, trying to remember what it had been like before the human tornado named A.J. had swept into his life. It had been much quieter, no question about it. And more orderly. Not to mention organized.

In other words, he realized with a jolt, it had been dull.

And to his surprise, dull wasn't nearly as appealing as it once had been.

"Okay, so we know the proposal has been presented by MacKenzie to the Board of Aldermen and the public hearing is scheduled for February 10. Is everyone planning to be there?" A.J. looked at her fellow merchants. Everyone was nodding assent. "Great. Now, let's talk about our plan for the meeting."

"I think we need a spokesperson for our group," Joe said.

"Good idea," Rose concurred. "I vote for you, A.J."

A.J. looked at her in surprise. "But I'm the new kid on the block. It might be better if one of you represented the group."

"But you're Jo's great niece, and she was the first one to come here. Now another generation is taking over. So you can speak for her and for yourself. I think you're the perfect choice," Steve replied.

"Steve is right," George agreed. "Jo would be our leader if she was here. So you should speak for us."

A.J. looked at the rest of the group. "How does everyone else feel about that? Carlos, Alene?"

"I'm fine with that," Carlos said.

"Me, too," chimed in Alene.

A.J. turned to Blake. He was still in the back, but at least he was sitting with the group this time. "Blake?"

"I agree with the consensus. I think you'd be great. And it would be a nice tribute to Jo."

"Well, if you're all sure…" A.J. looked down at her notes. "I think we need to have some residents speak, too."

"I already spoke to Mark Sanders, one of my regulars," Rose said. "He's an attorney, lives a couple of blocks away. He said he'd speak on our behalf."

"And I talked to Ellen Levine about it, too," Steve offered. "She grew up here, and she feels passionately about preserving the character of the area. And she's very grateful to people like us, who helped revitalize Maplewood. So she's willing to speak."

"A lot of people are planning to attend, too," Alene offered.

"Great. It sounds like everything's under control. If everyone will get me their petitions before the meeting, I'll present them when I speak. Anything else?" No one spoke, and A.J. nodded. "Okay. T minus twenty-one days and counting. Keep your fingers crossed!"

"Excuse me, miss. Could you tell me if Liam is working today?"

A.J. glanced up from the cash register and smiled at the woman with cobalt-blue eyes who was standing on the other side of the counter. There was something familiar about her, but A.J. couldn't quite put her finger on it. She appeared to be in her early-to-mid-fifties, and her long brown hair was pulled back into a single braid. A man with a nicely groomed salt-and-pepper beard stood behind her. It looked as if he could stand to lose a few pounds, but it was hard to tell because of their bulky winter coats.

"I'm sorry, there's no one here by that name," A.J. said. "Are you sure you have the right shop?"

"Jan, he doesn't use that name anymore, remember?" the man said.

The woman looked sheepish. "I know. But I always think of him that way. It's hard to…Liam!"

At the delighted look on her face, A.J. turned to follow her gaze. Blake stood in the doorway to the office. Shock was the only word to describe the expression on his face.

"How are you, son?"

Even after the man spoke, it took Blake a few moments to recover. "What are you doing here?"

"Paying you a surprise visit," the woman said, her delight undiminished by Blake's abrupt greeting and lack of enthusiasm.

"We're on our way to a convention in Chicago and thought we'd make a little detour, stop in and see how you are," the man spoke again.

Blake finally recovered enough to move forward, but he kept the counter between himself and his visitors. "You could have called first. I would have been more prepared."

"Then it wouldn't have been a surprise," the woman replied brightly.

Though A.J. stood mere inches away from him,

Blake seemed oblivious to her presence. And unsure how to proceed. So A.J. took charge. She stepped forward and held out her hand.

"Welcome to Turning Leaves. I'm A. J. Williams, Blake's partner."

The woman took her hand first. "I'm Jan Sullivan. This is my husband, Carl. We're Liam's...sorry, Blake's...parents."

"Nice to meet you," Blake's father said as he gave her hand a hearty squeeze. "You must be Jo's great niece. We were sorry to hear of her passing. She was a wonderful lady."

"Thank you." Since Blake still wasn't speaking, A.J. filled in the gap. "Did you just arrive?"

"Yes. We'd hoped to spend a couple of days in St. Louis, but we took an interesting detour or two on the way here that delayed us," Carl said. "So we'll need to leave tomorrow if we want to get to Chicago for the whole convention. But we couldn't come this close and not stop in to see Blake."

A.J. recalled that Blake had once told her his parents were from Oregon. She looked at Blake's father in surprise. "Did you drive all the way from the West Coast?"

"Yes. We love road trips. But we haven't had time to take many these past few years."

"This sure brings back a lot memories, doesn't it, Carl?" Blake's mother was looking around the shop, a smile of recollection on her lips.

"Yes, it does. That was a good summer for us. I see you've made some changes."

"When were you here last?" A.J. asked.

"Oh, it's been several years. I love the reading area in the front. It's so inviting," Jan said.

Finally Blake spoke. "Do you need a place to stay tonight?" The question was clearly prompted only out of a sense of obligation. He hadn't moved from behind the counter, and A.J. suspected that a whole lot more than a glass display case separated Blake and his parents.

"No, thank you, son. We already checked into a hotel."

Blake's relief was almost palpable. A.J. looked at him curiously—and with a certain degree of censure. His parents had obviously made a special trip to see him. Whatever their differences, surely he could afford to be hospitable for one night. And if he couldn't, she could, she decided.

On impulse, she spoke. "I don't want to impose on family time, but if you don't have any other plans for the evening, I'd be happy to offer you a home-cooked meal." She looked over at Blake. "You're invited, too, of course."

Blake stared at her as if she'd lost her mind.

"Why, thank you!" Jan replied. "But it's such short notice…I'm afraid it would be too much trouble."

"Not at all. Sometimes impromptu parties are the most fun."

"We couldn't agree more, right, Carl?"

"Absolutely."

"Unless Blake has other ideas, I think that sounds lovely," Jan said.

They all turned to Blake expectantly. It was clear he had no ideas at all.

"Blake, would you prefer to go out to dinner somewhere with just your mom and dad?" A.J. prompted when the silence lengthened.

If looks could kill, A.J. would be history. But she tilted her chin up and steadily returned his glare.

"Dinner at your place sounds fine." Blake ground out the words through clenched teeth.

A.J. ignored Blake and turned back to his parents with a cheery smile. "Terrific. Let me write down the directions for you. I'm sure you're tired, so we'll make it early."

After exchanging a few more pleasantries, A.J. stepped away to help a customer, leaving Blake alone with his parents. She glanced his way a couple of times, but he never moved from behind the counter. And even from a distance, his stiff posture spoke eloquently. Had she made a mistake by inviting them all to dinner? There was clearly no love lost on Blake's side. Yet his parents obviously cared for him. She could see it in their eyes. So what was the story? Had she stepped into the middle of something she'd regret?

But it was too late for regrets. She'd told Blake once that she didn't waste time on them. Which was true. Better to think about the dinner to come.

Then again, maybe not, she admitted as she glanced back at the three people standing at the counter. Considering the obviously strained relationship between parents and son, this could prove to be a very long evening.

A.J. put a match to the final wick, taking a moment to enjoy the soft, warm glow from the flickering candles placed throughout the living room. On a cold January evening like this, a fireplace would be perfect. But apartments like hers didn't come with such amenities.

Still, she was pleased with what she'd been able to do with the small space. She'd supplemented the few things she'd brought from Chicago with garage-sale finds, and the overall effect was warm and inviting. A small dinette set stood in the eating alcove next to the galley-style kitchen, and she'd covered the table with a handmade woven blanket she'd brought back from the Middle East. More candles of various heights stood in the center.

The small couch in the living room was draped with a colorful throw, and she'd turned a small trunk with brass hinges into a coffee table. A bookcase displayed favorite volumes as well as small pieces of sculpture. The final touch had been a fresh coat of off-white paint, which had brightened the dingy tan walls considerably and offered a great backdrop for some of her native art.

With a satisfied nod, she went back to the kitchen to check on dinner. She hadn't made this couscous-based dish in quite a while, but for some reason she had a feeling that Jan and Carl would appreciate it. She wasn't so sure about Blake.

She frowned as she stirred brown rice into the pot. She wasn't sure about him in a lot of ways, actually. He'd avoided her the rest of the afternoon, busying himself with customers in the shop or calling patrons whose orders had come in. She wouldn't have been surprised if he'd backed out of her invitation. In fact, when she finally cornered him to tell him she was leaving a little early to get dinner started, she was fully prepared for him to say he wasn't coming. But he didn't. He just gave her a curt nod and turned away.

If she'd made a huge faux pas, she was sorry. But she had taken an immediate liking to Jan and Carl. And in the face of their son's lack of hospitality, she'd felt compelled to step in and show some Christian charity. After all, they'd made a big detour to visit Blake. If he chose not to appreciate it, that was his issue. At least *she* could be friendly.

The doorbell rang, and A.J. put a lid on the pot, then wiped her hands on a towel. Let the games begin, she thought with a wry grin as she went to welcome her guests.

Despite Blake's buttoned-up style and obsession with punctuality, she'd half expected him to show up late for dinner in an attempt to shave as many minutes as possible off the evening. But instead she found him waiting on the other side of the door.

At her surprised look, he glanced at his watch. "Am I early?"

"No. Come in, *Liam*." She hoped her kidding tone would lighten the mood, but it had the opposite effect.

He didn't move. "That's not funny."

The teasing light in her eyes faded. "Sorry. Guess I hit a nerve."

"I don't use that name."

"Why not?"

"It's…weird."

"No, it isn't. It's very popular."

"It wasn't when I was a kid."

She eyed him thoughtfully. "When I was a kid, there was a little girl in our class named Maude. She got teased a lot. Is that what happened to you?"

"Worse. Boys aren't that nice."

"Surely your friends stood up for you?"

He looked at her for a moment, as if silently debating how to respond, but in the end ignored her comment. "Blake is my mother's maiden name—and my middle name. I've been using it since I was twelve. Now, do you think I could come in? It's a little drafty out here."

"Of course." She stepped back, instantly contrite, and ushered him in. "Let me take your coat."

He shrugged out of his leather jacket and handed it to her.

"Make yourself comfortable. I'll be right back."

She disappeared down a hall, and Blake took a moment to look over the tiny apartment. He didn't live extravagantly, but her living room, dining area and kitchen could easily fit into his great room, with space left over. And her decor—eclectic was probably the kindest word to describe it. Nothing seemed to match. Yet, oddly enough, it all blended. There was a slight Middle Eastern feel to the room, but he couldn't say exactly why. Maybe it was the artwork that hung on the walls, or the patterns in the fabrics. But he had to admit it was pleasant. And comfortable. And homey—which was not a word he could use for his own house. It might be bigger, and the furniture might match, but even after two years it didn't feel like a home.

A wife and children might help. And they were certainly in his plans. Had been for some time, in fact. He just hadn't met the right woman yet. But he knew exactly who he was looking for. June Cleaver. He wanted a homemaker—in the best sense of the word. A woman who made her family a priority, who might work outside the home but never forgot that home was what counted most. Someone who understood the importance of settling down, building a life in one place, becoming part of a community. He was not interested in returning to the vagabond, gypsy lifestyle he'd once known.

"Can I offer you something to drink?"

Blake turned as A.J. reentered the room. Speaking of gypsies, she kind of looked like one tonight. She was wearing something…different. So what else was new? he thought wryly. The full-length garment was made of a shimmery, patterned fabric in shades of green, purple and royal blue. It was nipped in at the waist with a wide belt, and swirled gracefully around her legs as she walked. It wasn't exactly his idea of dine-at-home attire. But it did look…festive. And suddenly he felt underdressed.

"I didn't have time to change," he said, half-apologetic, half-defensive.

She gazed at him. He'd obviously come directly from the shop, though it was clear he'd taken time to freshen up. His clean-shaven jaw showed no evidence of afternoon shadow.

A.J. shrugged. "No need. It's just a casual evening."

"You don't look casual."

She grinned. "I probably look weird to you."

He felt his neck grow warm. "I didn't say that."

"You didn't have to. I've worked with you practically every day for almost two months, Blake." He noted that she was careful to use his preferred name. "I quickly realized that you're a pretty conventional guy."

"You mean stuffy."

"I didn't say that," she parroted his words back to him.

"I've worked with you for almost two months, too. I think I have a pretty good idea what your opinion is of me," he countered.

"Really? You might be surprised."

"I don't think so."

"No? Okay, try this on for size. I think you are an extraordinarily capable and bright guy. I have no doubt Aunt Jo would have been in bankruptcy long ago without your help. Your attention to detail is fantastic, and you're absolutely one hundred percent reliable. You don't like change, but in our current situation that's probably a plus. Since I know you'll question anything I propose, I think things through even more carefully than I otherwise might. You're very disciplined and regimented, which are good things in moderation. But if you'll pardon one editorial comment, you might enjoy life a little more if you added a dash of spontaneity. So how did I do?"

Blake stared at the woman across from him. She'd pretty much nailed him. And been diplomatic in the process. She'd complimented his good points, and even put a positive spin on the qualities she clearly didn't admire.

"Not bad," he acknowledged grudgingly.

"Come on, Blake, admit it. I was right on the money," she teased. "Now it's your turn."

"What do you mean?"

"Tell me how you see me."

"I didn't say I wanted to play this game."

"Too late. I took my turn. Now it's yours. And then I'll tell you how close you came."

Blake felt cornered. But it was clear A.J. wasn't going to let him off the hook. She'd settled into a corner of the couch, tucked her leg under her, and looked prepared to wait as long as it took for him to take his turn.

"You aren't…what I expected," he hedged.

She shook her head. "Not good enough. Try again."

"You're…different."

"Different how?"

He raked his fingers through his hair and jammed his other hand into the pocket of his slacks. "Look, I'm no good at this let-it-all-hang-out kind of thing."

She considered him for a moment. "Okay, then let me give it a try, and you can tell me if what I *think* you think is actually true. How's that?"

Did he even have a choice?

"At first, you thought I was going to be some airhead without any business sense. The M.B.A. surprised you. And made you a little more comfortable. But you still consider me somewhat of an intruder, and you feel like I've invaded your turf. Although you haven't liked the changes I've made, you've had to admit that they've paid off—for the most part. Which bothers you. You think I have weird taste. And I most certainly do not fit your image of the ideal woman. How's that?"

She was good. He'd give her that. "Close."

She rolled her eyes. "For a man who deals with the written word, you sure don't communicate much. Which might be a problem if you ever do find that ideal woman."

He glared at her. How had the conversation suddenly taken such a personal turn? "How do you know I haven't?" he retorted.

"Haven't what?"

"Found the ideal woman."

She shrugged. "Just a guess."

Before he could respond, she made a move to stand, but for a moment she seemed to have trouble getting the leg she'd tucked under her to cooperate. When she finally got to her feet, she winced slightly and took a moment to steady herself on the back of the couch.

Blake frowned. It wasn't like her to be so awkward. Even though she was tall, she always moved with a lithe grace. "Is something wrong?"

She shook her head. "No. I know better than to sit like that. It was my own fault. So, can I get you that drink now?"

What was her own fault? That she had to struggle to stand? And why had she struggled? The question was on the tip of his tongue, but he bit it back, recalling how he'd balked when she'd gotten personal. She would have every right to do the same. After all, they were only business associates. Short-term, at that. So he let it pass.

"A white soda, if you have it."

"Of course. I'll be right back."

He watched as she made the short trip to the kitchen, noting that her gait didn't seem quite normal. But she was clearly doing her best to hide it.

Blake knew he should just put her personal problem out of his mind. He needed to worry about making it through this evening with his parents, not about A.J.'s physical difficulties. She was an independent woman, clearly capable of taking care of herself. She didn't need his concern. In fact, she might even resent it.

But as Blake looked around the cozy third-floor apartment and recalled the three sets of stairs he'd had to climb to reach her door, he couldn't help but wonder if she was having trouble negotiating them. Especially juggling bags of groceries. Or a basket of laundry. And if she was, was there anyone she could call on for help?

Blake didn't think so. Her two sisters were far away. And though she'd made many acquaintances since arriving in St. Louis, those were all new friendships. Not the sort of long-established relationships where one felt comfortable asking for favors. And she'd never mentioned a boyfriend—or even a close female friend—that she'd left behind in Chicago.

So maybe he and A.J. did have something in common after all. Though their philosophies of life might be radically different, and they might disagree on pretty much everything, it seemed they shared one trait.

They were both alone.

Chapter Five

"**A.J.**, this is fabulous!" Carl helped <u>himself</u> to a second serving of the main dish.

"Thank you. But I'm glad I didn't know your background this afternoon. I would have been too intimidated to invite you."

"You can cook for me any day. And I'm hoping I can wrangle this recipe out of you. It would be a perfect dish to feature in one of our cooking demonstrations."

"I'll be happy to share it. After all, I wouldn't have it if someone hadn't shared it with me. But tell me more about your store. How long have you had it?"

"It seems like forever, but actually it's only been fifteen years. It took us quite a while to find our niche, but better late than never, I guess," Jan chimed in with a laugh. "We'd always had an interest in good food, so opening a natural food shop just seemed…well, natural."

"My grandfather was a chef, so I already had a lot

of training in food prep," Carl added. "But I went to culinary school while Jan got her credentials as a dietitian. Then the whole thing just took off. Besides running the shop, Jan does seminars on the principles of healthy eating and I do the hands-on cooking demonstrations that put those principles into action. It's a lot of fun."

"And a lot of work," Jan added. "Especially since we opened a second shop a few months ago."

"You have two shops now?" Blake spoke for the first time since they'd gathered at the table. His tone was incredulous.

"We're as amazed as you are," Carl affirmed. "We got into this business because we thought we'd enjoy it. We never expected to make a lot of money. But we've been successful far beyond our wildest dreams."

"The only trouble with success is that it eats into your flexibility and freedom," Jan said with a sigh, helping herself to a second slice of homemade whole grain bread. "We used to love to take road trips. But this is the first time in years that we've been able to get away for any length of time."

Out of the corner of her eye, A.J. saw Blake reach for a second helping of the entrée to supplement the meager first serving he'd taken. When she'd presented the unusual vegetarian dish, she could see the wariness on his face. You'd think she'd been asking him to eat worms, she thought wryly. The man's eating habits were obviously not adventurous. He was clearly as cautious with food as he was with people. And maybe with life.

"So tell us where you got this recipe, A.J.," Jan encouraged.

"In Afghanistan."

That got everyone's attention.

"You've been to Afghanistan?" Blake shot her a startled look.

She nodded. "I lived there for almost three years."

"Good grief! And we thought *we'd* lived in some exotic places," Jan said.

"What were you doing there?" Carl asked.

A.J. hesitated. "It's kind of a long story. And maybe not the best dinner conversation."

"We'd really like to hear it, A.J. And we have all evening," Jan assured her.

A.J. looked at the faces around the table. Jan and Carl seemed genuinely interested. Blake seemed a bit stunned.

"Well, I can give you the highlights," she agreed.

And for the next hour, as they finished every last bite of the main dish and put a good dent in the Middle Eastern honey-based puff-pastry dessert that followed, she regaled them with tales of her time in Afghanistan as they plied her with questions.

A.J. told them of her work in two small villages and at a clinic. Of the kindness of the people, despite their abject poverty. Of hardships almost beyond comprehension. Of the lack of warmth and shelter and food. Of malnutrition and starvation. She described one young child, eighteen months old, who was just twenty-seven inches long and weighed only eleven pounds when she was brought to the clinic.

"She was starving to death," A.J. said, her voice slightly unsteady. "She was the youngest of six children. Their parents had both died, and their grandmother took care of them. They lived with dozens of other families in the skeleton of a bombed-out building. The grandmother did her best, but she had to rely on begging to put food on the table, and she wasn't always successful.

"If she had waited two more days to bring Zohra to the clinic, the little girl would have died. But even though her grandmother got her there in time, we were understaffed and had very limited resources. So in order for Zohra to have any chance at all, her grandmother needed to stay and give her routine care, like bathing and feeding. But there were five other children to take care of, too.

"We put a call in to Good Samaritan, and they were able to provide enough funding to cover Zohra's hospital stay and pay someone to stay with the other children while Zohra's grandmother cared for her at the clinic. That story had a happy ending...but so many others didn't."

A.J. grew silent, and Blake saw her struggling to control the tears that suddenly welled in her eyes. For some strange reason, he wanted to reach for her hand. Comfort her. Enfold those delicate fingers protectively in his. Which made no sense. They were co-workers. Nothing more. So he stifled the impulse and kept his hands in his lap.

His mother was less restrained. She reached over and laid her hand on A.J.'s. "That is an incredible story," she said in a hushed voice. "How did you deal with it, day after day?"

A.J. drew a deep breath and gave her a shaky smile. "Not every day was that emotional. It was very hard work under very primitive conditions, but the people had a great capacity for joy even in the face of tragedy and sorrow. And they were so grateful for our support. Most of the artwork you see in my apartment was given to me as thank-you gifts. It was an incredibly rewarding experience."

"But weren't you ever frightened? Afghanistan isn't the safest place," Jan said.

"No. I really wasn't. I'd prayed a lot about the decision before I went, and by the time I actually got on the plane, I knew with absolute conviction that that was where God wanted me to be at that point in my life. So I just put my trust in Him."

"I take it Good Samaritan is a Christian organization?"

A.J. turned to Carl. "Yes. But not blatantly so. By that I mean that we didn't focus on converting anyone to Christianity. We answered questions, of course, if people asked. And they knew we were Christian. But our witness to our faith was more through actions than words."

"Which is the way it should be," Carl affirmed. "Wasn't it Francis of Assisi who told people to spread the Gospel, and to use words only if all else failed?"

Blake stared at his father. "Since when have you been interested in religion?"

Carl glanced at Jan. "We've been going to church for

a number of years, Blake. Another thing we discovered a little later in life."

"That's one of our regrets, actually," Jan said. "God wasn't part of our lives when you were growing up. We didn't give you much of a foundation for faith."

While Blake was trying to digest this news, Jan turned back to A.J. "So what made you leave? Did you eventually burn out?"

"No. I got a pretty serious intestinal parasite that just wouldn't respond to treatment. So I had to come back for medical care. It actually took months to get rid of the pesky thing. At that point Good Samaritan was reluctant to send me back because they were afraid my health had been compromised. I was fine, and the doctors all gave me a good report, but the organization preferred I stay in the States and work out of its Chicago headquarters. That's where I was before I came to St. Louis."

Carl shook his head. "That's an amazing story. It kind of puts our adventures to shame, doesn't it, Jan?"

She nodded. "I admire you, A.J. What you did was so selfless. You got right into the thick of it, took an active role in trying to make the world a better place. Even in our activist days, we just attended rallies, marched and asked people to sign petitions."

"That's more than a lot of people do," A.J. reassured her. "In fact, we're sort of engaging in that kind of battle right now with the bookshop."

"Why? What's going on?" Carl asked.

After A.J. explained the situation, Jan leaned forward, an expression of concern on her face. "Is there anything we can do to help? Jo worked so hard to keep the character of the neighborhood intact, and to revitalize the area. So have all the merchants. I'd hate for that to change."

"I appreciate the offer. But everyone's very committed to telling our story and supporting our cause. I think we've done everything we can so far. We'll turn out in force at the Board of Aldermen meeting in a couple of weeks. And if that doesn't work…well, we can always take more dramatic measures. One of the merchants has a contact in the media."

"Media coverage is always good," Carl said with a nod. "Don't be afraid to use it. But you'll need to have an event of some kind to catch their interest—a protest march or something."

A.J. risked a sidelong glance at Blake. The look of distaste on his face was almost comical. "We'll keep that in mind," she told Carl.

"Well, if you need us to do anything, let us know. We used to get involved in these kinds of things all the time."

"I will. Now, would anyone like more coffee?"

Carl glanced at his watch regretfully. "I'd love some, but if we're going to get an early start tomorrow, we ought to call it a night."

"A.J., we can't thank you enough for this wonderful evening," Jan said warmly.

"It was truly my pleasure."

She retrieved their coats, then followed them to the door. Blake stood slightly apart, his hands in his pockets.

"Drive safely," A.J. said.

"We will."

There was a moment of awkward silence, then Carl held his hand out to Blake. "Take care, son."

Blake stepped forward and took it. "You, too."

Jan moved toward him and held out her arms. He hesitated, then returned her hug awkwardly. "Will you stay in touch?" There was a wistful quality in her voice that tugged at A.J.'s heart.

"Of course."

When she turned back to A.J., her eyes looked damp and her smile was a little too bright. "Thank you again for a lovely meal."

Impulsively A.J. stepped forward and gave each of them a hug. "You're very welcome. Please stop by any time you're in St. Louis."

She waved them off at the door, then turned. She'd also retrieved Blake's coat, expecting him to follow closely on the heels of his parents. But he was still standing in the same place, a frown marring his brow. She hesitated a moment, but when he made no move to leave, she closed the door.

"Can I offer you something else, Blake?"

"No." Actually, that was a lie. She *could* offer him something—answers. Starting with how she had managed to create a better rapport with his parents in the first thirty minutes of their visit than he had in thirty years of life.

"Well, go ahead and make yourself comfortable. I'm just going to blow out the candles on the table and put away the perishables. Then I'll join you."

When A.J. returned, cradling a mug of tea, Blake had

claimed one of the side chairs. She sat at right angles to him on the couch, but he noted that she was careful not to tuck her leg under her this time. She'd mentioned the intestinal parasite. But had she been injured in some other way in Afghanistan that she hadn't shared? Or was the leg injury more recent?

"Your parents are great, Blake," she said, forcing him to refocus his thoughts.

"I'm glad you think so."

She looked at him curiously. "Obviously you don't."

"I didn't exactly have an ideal childhood."

"By ideal do you mean typical? Or perfect?"

"It was neither."

"Tell me about it."

He shrugged. "You've met my parents. And you're good at that mind-reading game you were playing earlier. I'm sure you can put two and two together."

Thoughtfully she took a sip of her tea. "I have a feeling your parents might have been hippies in their younger days."

"Give the lady a gold star."

At his sarcastic tone she tilted her head and looked at him. When she spoke, there was no censure in her tone. "Is that a bad thing? Were they into the drugs-and-free-sex scene?"

"No. But they were always fighting for some cause. Attending rallies, going on marches, the whole nine yards. Or they were trying out alternative lifestyles. We even spent one summer in a commune. You know how most people think of a certain place when they hear the word home? I don't. We were never in one place long enough."

"I guess I've always thought of home not so much as a place, but as simply being with the people you love," A.J. said mildly, without reproach.

"That's easy to say if you weren't the one uprooted every few months." There was bitterness in his voice now. And anger, simmering just below the surface. As if it had been there a long time. "I was in a new school practically every year—sometimes twice a year. I was never in one place long enough to make friends. To join the Boy Scouts. To play on a soccer team. It's a pretty lonely life for a kid."

And for the adult that kid became, she thought. The effects of his isolated childhood were clearly evident in the man across from her.

"But your parents seem to love you," she pointed out.

He sighed. "They do, in their own way. But I think I was very unplanned, and they just decided early on that my arrival wasn't going to put a crimp in their lifestyle. So they dragged me all over the country with them. They picked up odd jobs wherever they went, but it was always hit or miss. They had an easy-come, easy-go attitude that seemed to suit them. I was always the one who worried about whether we'd have enough food on the table. Or a place to spend the night. Even as a little kid."

"Did you? Have enough food, and a place to spend the night, I mean."

He thought about the time they'd almost gone to a homeless shelter, but at the last minute his dad had found work. "Yes. But it was always feast or famine, depending on whether my parents were working. I never knew where our next meal was coming from. Or where I'd be sleeping. And I hated that."

Which explained a lot, A.J. thought. Now she better understood Blake's dislike of change, his need for predictability. "So how did you meet Aunt Jo?"

His face relaxed, and a slight smile lifted the corners of his mouth. "We were in St. Louis one summer, right after Jo opened the shop. I don't even remember why we were there. Anyway, she hired Dad to do some work. I went with him every day, and she sort of took me under her wing. For that one summer at least, there was stability in my life. She was the best friend I'd ever had. And we never lost touch. So when the shop was on shaky ground financially three years ago, I was happy to come and help out."

"What were you doing before that?" Blake was always so close-mouthed about himself that A.J. wondered if he'd take offense at her question. But he answered easily.

"Investment banking. In Chicago."

She raised her eyebrows. "You gave that up to run a bookstore?"

"Initially, I just took a leave of absence. I wasn't sure I'd stay. But I was getting tired of the international travel and the long hours, even though the money was great. After I was here for a few weeks, I discovered I liked the book business. And St. Louis. So I stayed."

It made sense to A.J.—St. Louis, with its Midwestern values and small-town feel, was surely a world away from the nonconformist lifestyle he knew as a child. And the town also held happy memories for him. "I'm sure Aunt Jo was very grateful for your help."

He shrugged. "It was small repayment for all she gave me. Including that great summer in St. Louis. That was the first time in my life that I felt like I belonged somewhere. She gave me more of a sense of family than my parents ever did."

The bitter edge was back in his voice. A.J. finished her tea and set the cup on the chest. When she spoke, her voice was sympathetic. "I can see how growing up like that would be tough," she said.

Blake looked at her warily. "I'm surprised you're not rushing to my parents' defense. You got along with them famously."

"They seem like great people," she affirmed. "But they're probably different now than they were twenty-five years ago. We all learn and grow and change. Maybe they'd do things differently if they had a second chance. Maybe not. Maybe they thought the life they gave you was the right one at the time. But in any case, you can't change the past. And it seems to me that they'd very much like you to be part of their future."

"It's a little late."

"It doesn't have to be. They obviously love you, Blake. I think they'd like to reconnect, if you'd just let them in."

Deep inside, he knew that A.J. was right. His parents did love him. Maybe they hadn't demonstrated that love the way he'd needed them to as a youngster, but he'd never doubted that they cared for him. And he knew that with a little encouragement they would welcome him back into their lives. He was the stumbling block. His resentment ran so deep, and the chasm between them was so wide and of such long duration that he wasn't sure it could be breached. For a reconciliation to work, he'd have to find a way to forgive them. And in all honesty, he wasn't sure he was up to the task.

A.J. sat quietly, watching him, her eyes telling him silently that she understood his dilemma. She had certainly disproved his first impression of her as a ditzy airhead, he admitted. Instead, she was smart, insightful, empathetic—and beautiful. He'd been noticing that more and more lately. Hers wasn't a dramatic, model-like beauty. It was quieter than that. And deeper. It was the kind of beauty that gave a face dimension and character and soul. When you looked into A.J.'s eyes, you knew that she was a strong woman. A survivor. A woman with deep convictions who would stand beside the people she loved. In good times and bad.

A startled look flashed across Blake's face. Now where had *that* phrase come from? He certainly didn't think of A.J. in that way. True, he'd never met anyone quite like her. She was…interesting. And she was easy to talk to. He'd never told anyone as much about his past in one sitting as he had tonight. She would definitely make someone a good wife. But not him.

Blake stood, and A.J. seemed surprised by his abrupt movement. She quickly followed suit, and he was relieved to note that she didn't struggle this time.

"I need to leave. It's getting late."

"Okay." She reached for his coat, studying him while he shrugged into it. He'd been quiet for so long after her last comment that she was beginning to think she'd overstepped her bounds. He wasn't a man given to personal revelations, and she'd pushed him pretty hard tonight about his parents. His jaw was set in a firm line, and twin furrows still creased his brows. He definitely did not look like a happy camper. Maybe she needed to make amends.

"Blake, I'm sorry if I said anything to offend you."

He gazed at her, his cobalt-colored eyes guarded. "You didn't."

She put her hands on her hips and studied him. "Why am I not buying that?"

He turned up the collar of his jacket and sighed. "Look, A.J., this is the first time in years that I've spent a whole evening with my parents. I'm still trying to process everything that happened. Cut me some slack, okay?"

"Sure."

She walked with him to the door, where he turned. "Thank you for dinner."

"You're welcome."

Her tone was more subdued, and her eyes looked troubled. He felt an urge to reach out and touch her, just as he had at the dinner table. Again he stifled it, jamming his fists into the pockets of his jacket. "I mean that. Everything was really good."

The ghost of a smile whispered around her lips. "I thought you were going to have a fit when you found out the main dish was vegetarian."

His own lips lifted in a smile. "I probably shouldn't have been surprised. Knowing you. But I enjoyed it."

"See? Sometimes it pays to take a chance and try something new."

"Maybe," he conceded.

"Be careful on your way to the car," she cautioned.

He was glad she'd brought that up. Though signs of turnaround were evident, he hadn't been impressed by the run-down neighborhood.

"I will. This isn't the safest area."

She frowned. "I was talking about the ice."

"Oh. Well, I'll watch for that, too. But this isn't the best part of the city. I hope you're cautious, as well, especially at night."

"I spent three years in Afghanistan, remember? Caution is my middle name. Besides, this area seems fine to me. The Realtor said it was turning around."

"It still has a long way to go."

She tilted her head. "Let me guess. You live in suburbia, in a house with a white picket fence."

At her accurate conclusion, he felt hot color steal up his neck. "I don't have to defend my lifestyle."

She shrugged. "Neither do I. This suits me fine. And it suits my budget even better."

How did this woman continually manage to outwit him? He'd always been good at thinking on his feet, but she was even better. Especially now, when his brain was reeling from all he'd learned this evening—about his parents' second shop, A.J.'s sojourn in Afghanistan and his own feelings about his childhood. It was time to call it a night.

"I'll see you tomorrow, A.J.," he said, suddenly weary.

"See you, Blake."

As the door shut behind him and he started the trek down the three flights of steps, he realized he still didn't know what had caused A.J. that awkward, obviously painful moment as she rose from the couch.

And he also realized that he hadn't asked the one question he'd been most interested in during her stories about Afghanistan. She'd spent several years earning an M.B.A. from one of the toughest schools in the country. She'd obviously intended to pursue a business career.

Why had she scrapped those plans to go to Afghanistan?

"What time does the bus leave, A.J.?"

A.J. glanced at her watch before responding to Nancy. "Not until four. We should arrive by nine in the morning."

"I wish I could go."

"You have a little one to take care of here. God understands."

"I'll be with all of you in spirit."

"We know. And thanks for filling in for me tonight."

"It's the least I could do."

"I have all my stuff in the car, so I don't need to leave until three."

"Don't put yourself in a bind. Go whenever you need to," Nancy assured her.

Blake overheard the last part of the conversation as he arrived at the front counter. He turned to A.J. as Nancy went to assist a customer. "You're leaving early?"

"Yes. Is that a problem? Nancy will be here. And tomorrow is my Saturday off."

"I wanted to go over the list of new releases before I placed the order."

"Can it wait until Monday?"

"I guess it will have to."

A.J. knew he was aggravated that she hadn't told him of her early departure. But it had been a last-minute decision. She hadn't been sure she could force herself to make another church-sponsored bus trip. In the end, though, she'd felt compelled to go because the cause was so important. "Sorry for the short notice on this, Blake. I didn't decide about this trip until yesterday."

"You're going on vacation?"

"Hardly. I'm going with a church group to Washington for the annual pro-life march. A lot of area churches are sending buses."

He frowned. "You're going to a protest?"

She studied him. Her trip probably reminded him of the rallies and marches his parents had participated in when he was a child. "It's not exactly a protest. It's just a peaceful march to let our legislators know that a lot of people have serious concerns about abortion."

He glanced out the window, at the bleak January landscape. "It's going to be cold in Washington."

"My body may be cold. But my heart will be warm."

"Is it really worth going all that way just to make a point?"

She looked at him steadily. "Not everything is worth fighting for, Blake. But when it comes to saving innocent lives, I want my voice to be heard."

A customer came up just then, and A.J. turned to assist him. Blake watched her walk away, chatting animatedly with the man, then glanced out the window once again. He couldn't think of anything more unappealing than riding all night on a bus, marching for hours in the cold, then riding home on the bus again. He'd rather compete in two marathons back-to-back than do that.

But A.J. wasn't doing this because it was comfortable. She was doing it because she believed that it was right. He'd never met anyone with such sincere convictions. His parents had always been rallying behind different causes, and they'd been passionate about them at the time, but then they'd moved on to something else. Their passions were fleeting. And more on the surface. A.J.'s went deep. And seemed to be long-lasting. And completely unselfish.

Blake admired that. But it also made him a little uncomfortable. Because somehow he didn't feel that he measured up. Sure, he had causes that he believed in. That's why he was the treasurer for a local homeless shelter, why he served on the board of directors of the local Big Brothers organization. But he didn't have to get his hands dirty to do that. He wasn't in the trenches. He hadn't made a personal investment, like A.J. was making this weekend. Or like she'd made in Afghanistan. Maybe his convictions just weren't as strong as hers.

And there was no question about the strength of her conviction about abortion. He'd never really thought about the issue too deeply before. It was easier to buy into the woman's-right-to-choose opinion. It was easier not to get involved. It was easier not to take a stand.

But A.J. didn't go for the easy way out.

And maybe he shouldn't, either.

Blake looked around the shop, which had been transformed since A.J.'s arrival. She'd rearranged so many things. Including his life.

And he had a feeling she wasn't done yet.

Chapter Six

A.J. groaned and fumbled for the alarm clock, intent on stilling the persistent, jarring ring. It couldn't possibly be Monday morning already! But when she squinted bleary-eyed at the clock, the digital display confirmed that it was.

With a sigh, she sank back against her pillow and stole a few extra moments under the downy warmth of the fluffy comforter. In the past seventy-two hours, she was lucky if she'd managed more than twelve hours of fitful slumber. She hadn't been able to find a comfortable sleeping position in the bus on the way to Washington. But she'd figured she'd be so tired after standing for hours in the cold that she'd have no problem sleeping Saturday night on the way home.

However, that theory was never put to the test. Because only a couple of hours into their return journey they'd had to pull into a truck stop when light snow suddenly turned into a blizzard. And they'd been stuck there until Sunday morning. They hadn't gone hungry, but sleep was difficult. When they'd finally resumed their trip, many of the people were so exhausted that they slept all day. But by that time, A.J.'s hip was feeling the effects of the march, the cold and the confined conditions. She'd had to keep standing to prevent her muscles from cramping.

A.J. didn't normally think much about the accident and its aftereffects. But today it was hard not to, when her hip was throbbing so painfully. Carefully, she turned over and scrunched her pillow under her head. Even after eight years, the nightmare was still vivid in her mind. She closed her eyes, swallowing as the memories engulfed her, willing her frantic pulse to slow.

Dear Lord, please stay with me, she prayed. *Please see me through this dark moment, like You always do. Help me to feel Your care and Your love. To know that I'm not alone. Help me to be strong and to accept Your will, even when I don't understand it. To trust in You and not be afraid. Help me deal with the pain and the loneliness. Let me feel the warmth of Your presence, especially today, when I am hurting and the memories are so vivid.*

Slowly, A.J.'s breathing returned to normal and she gradually released the comforter that was bunched in her fists. It had been a long time since the pain had been so stark. Not just the pain from her hip, but the pain of loss. For a few moments it had felt so fresh, so intense, so raw. Prompted, she was sure, by the bus trip this weekend and the blizzard. But she'd get through this. God hadn't deserted her before. He wouldn't now. She might be exhausted and hurting and shaken by the flood of memories, but she'd been through worse. Far worse. She could make it through today.

And tomorrow would be better.

By Wednesday, A.J. had caught up on some sleep, and the burning pain in her hip had diminished to a dull throb. She was beginning to feel human again.

But Blake didn't see it that way. He'd been watching her since her return, and she didn't look good. There were dark smudges under her eyes, and she was limping. But she'd brushed off his careful questions, assuring him she was fine. Obviously, she wasn't going to talk.

But he figured Nancy might. A.J. confided in her. So she was his best source for information.

"Blake, when you have a minute could you help me move that box in the back that just came in? I need to check on a special order for a customer, and it's blocking the computer."

He turned to Nancy. Perfect timing. "Sure. Be right there."

When Blake joined her, she gave him an apologetic look. "Sorry to interrupt you while you were with a customer. Normally I would have asked A.J. But I didn't want to bother her. She still looks so tired."

"Yeah, I noticed. What happened?"

"Didn't she tell you? They ran into a snowstorm on the way back to St. Louis and had to spend Saturday night in a truck stop. So they drove all day Sunday to get home. I doubt she had much sleep from Friday morning to Sunday night."

That explained the dark circles under her eyes. But what about the limp?

"Did she hurt her leg on the trip?"

"Not that I know of. Why?"

"Haven't you noticed her limping?"

"No. Is she?"

He shrugged. "Maybe it was my imagination."

But it wasn't. The limp had been pronounced on Monday. However, Nancy had been off that day. By Tuesday, A.J. was managing to hide it pretty well. Today it was hardly discernible. Most people wouldn't notice. But he could see it. As well as the fine lines of strain around her mouth that told him she was in pain. And that bothered him. A lot.

By Friday, A.J. not only still looked tired, she had a doozy of a cold. Her nose was red and running, her cheeks were flushed and she had a hacking cough. Twice he urged her to go home. Both times she refused.

"I'll be fine," she said. "I'm not going to let a little thing like a cold slow me down."

And she didn't. She made it until closing, through sheer grit and determination. Blake admired her spunk—but not her stubbornness—and told her so. And for the first time in their acquaintance, he saw evidence of her Irish temper.

"Just leave me alone, Blake, okay?" she said angrily. "I've taken care of myself for years. I know what I'm capable of. I don't need any advice."

He was so taken aback by her abrupt tone that for a moment he was speechless. Then he felt his own temper begin to simmer. "Fine. Suit yourself." He turned on his heel and left.

A.J. was immediately sorry for her rudeness. And she was even sorrier when she woke up on Saturday morning. It was her weekend to work, but she didn't even have the energy to get out of bed. Calling Nancy wasn't an option because she was throwing a birthday party for Eileen. Which left Blake.

A.J. groaned. She doubted whether he would be very receptive to her request after her curt behavior yesterday. But when her temperature registered a hundred and one, she knew she had to try.

He startled her by answering on the first ring. At his clipped greeting, she hesitated.

"Hello?" he repeated, this time with an edge of impatience.

"Blake, it's A.J. Have I caught you at a bad time?"

He frowned. If she hadn't identified herself, he would never have recognized the thin, raspy voice on the other end of the line. "I was just heading out the door. What's wrong?"

She took a deep breath. "You were right yesterday, and I apologize for my short temper. I should have gone home. Because now I'm worse. Listen, I know this is really short notice, and it sounds like you already have other plans, but is there any way you can fill in for me at the shop today? Or part of the day? I'd call Nancy, but she's busy with Eileen's birthday party."

Blake glanced at his watch. He was due at a finance meeting for the homeless shelter in half an hour, and he had a Big Brothers board meeting at one o'clock.

There was no way he could get out of those commitments. Both groups were counting on him.

"I'm sorry, A.J. I can't. I'm already running late for one meeting, and I have another one after that."

Her heart sank. But what did she expect? Blake lived a structured life. Flexibility wasn't in his vocabulary. Last-minute changes would wreak havoc with his carefully made plans.

"Okay. I understand. I wouldn't want to disrupt your schedule. Thanks anyway."

"I'd help you out if I could."

"Like I said, I understand. Have a good day."

Before he could respond, she hung up. A muscle in his jaw twitched, and he put his own phone back in its base with more force than necessary. Her implication had been clear. He was too rigid to adjust his schedule to accommodate an emergency. She'd judged him without even asking the details of his refusal, which made him mad. So, fine. Let her deal with this predicament on her own. She'd brought it on herself, anyway, with her impromptu trip to Washington. She'd told him yesterday she could take care of herself. Well, today she'd have to.

Except that he couldn't get her out of his mind. Twice at the finance meeting he'd had to ask someone to repeat a question. And at the Big Brothers meeting he looked at his watch so many times that the president finally made a comment about it—and he was only half joking. By the time the meeting ended at three-thirty, Blake had made up his mind. He had to relieve A.J. at the shop. If she looked half as bad as she'd sounded that morning, she was probably about ready to drop.

In fact, she looked worse. After entering the shop from the rear, through the office, he paused on the threshold of the main room. A.J. was checking out a customer, but she was sitting behind the counter on a stool, not standing as she always did. And when she reached for a bag, he could see her hand shaking.

In several long strides he was beside her. He took the bag from her almost before she realized he was there, and when their hands brushed briefly her fingers felt hot and dry. She gazed at him blankly, her eyes dull with fever.

"I'll finish up this sale," he said close to her ear. "Stay put."

A.J. didn't argue. Which told him that she was really sick.

He dispensed with the customer as quickly as he could, then turned to her. Her shoulders were drooped, and her face was flushed. "I got here as quickly as I could. Did you take your temperature this morning?"

She nodded.

"What was it?"

"A hundred and one."

He muttered something under his breath, then spoke aloud. "Why didn't you tell me that when you called?"

She tried to shrug, but the effort seemed to require more energy than she had. "Would it have made a difference?"

He expelled a frustrated sigh. "I'm not even going to answer that. Did you call the doctor?"

"It's just a bug."

He thought about another bug...the persistent parasite from Afghanistan. Which might have weakened her immune system, made her more susceptible to other bugs. He doubted she should take any chances. He considered arguing—then thought better of it. She was probably right, and he was probably overreacting. It was most likely just a virus. But if she wasn't a lot better in a day or two, then he'd argue. Right now she needed to rest. "Fine. I'll get your coat."

"Why?"

"I'm taking you home."

"There's no one to watch the shop."

"I'll put a sign in the window."

She stared at him. "We've never closed the shop in the middle of the day before."

"I guess there's a first time for everything."

"But…we might lose customers."

"They'll come back."

Suddenly she frowned. "You can't drive me. My car's here."

"You're in no condition to drive."

"Blake, I appreciate the offer, but I can get home on my own."

As if to demonstrate her point, she stood. Then lost the argument when she swayed. He grabbed her upper arms to steady her, and she closed her eyes.

"Maybe…maybe you better drive me after all," she said faintly.

When she lifted her eyelids, Blake's intense eyes were riveted on hers. There was concern in their depths—and in that brief, unguarded instant, an unexpected tenderness that made her breath catch in her throat. She was only inches from his solid chest, and his strong arms held her steadily, protectively. For a fleeting moment, A.J. wanted to step into his embrace, to lay her head on his broad shoulder, to feel his arms enfold and hold her. It was a startling impulse, surely brought on by her weakened condition. To counter it, she tried to step back. But he held her fast, and their gazes locked.

Blake stared at A.J. Despite her attempt to move away, he didn't want to let her go. He wanted to protect her. It was a primitive instinct, one he had never before experienced. He'd dated a fair amount, but no one had ever elicited this response. It was…weird. Especially since he and A.J. were simply business associates. They hardly liked each other.

Someone cleared his throat, and Blake and A.J. turned to find a customer waiting to be checked out. Reluctantly, Blake released her, but not before he gave her one more quick, searching gaze. "Are you steady enough to go get your coat?"

She nodded mutely. For some reason her voice had deserted her.

"Okay. I'll meet you in the back in five minutes."

As A.J. waited for him, she tried to figure out what had just happened between them. It was almost like… attraction. Which was crazy. They were nothing alike. In fact, they were completely opposite. And they clashed all the time. There was no basis for any chemistry. Oh, sure, Blake was a nice-looking guy. In fact, as Morgan would say, he was a hunk. But he wasn't her type. Whatever had happened out there had to be a fluke. Maybe it had something to do with her fever.

But that didn't quite ring true. Because based on what she'd seen in his eyes, A.J. was pretty sure that Blake had experienced the same thing.

And he wasn't sick.

Someone was using a hammer. In the middle of the night. A.J. pried her eyelids open and squinted at the clock. Seven o'clock. Okay, so maybe it wasn't the middle of the night after all. But it sure felt like it was.

The pounding started again. This time it was accompanied by Blake's voice, which had a slightly desperate edge.

"A.J.? Open the door! I'm calling the police if you don't!"

She struggled to her feet, favoring her hip, which had started to ache again. She limped to the door and fumbled with the locks in the darkness. When she finally pulled the door open, she caught a glimpse of Mr. Simmons, her elderly neighbor, peering through a crack in his door across the hall.

"Everything all right, A.J.?" he asked.

"Fine, thanks, Mr. Simmons. Sorry to bother you," she said hoarsely.

She stepped back, and as Blake came in she did some mental arithmetic. It was still an hour to closing. "Who's at the shop?"

"I called Nancy. The party ended at five-thirty and she came in." He flipped on a light and studied her. "How are you?"

"I took some aspirin. And I've been sleeping."

Which didn't answer his question. But her appearance said it all. Her eyes were watery and her face still looked flushed. "Have you taken your temperature lately?"

She shook her head. "Like I said, I've been sleeping."

"Why don't you go do that while I reheat this soup?"

She stared at the bag in this hand. "You brought me soup?"

"I figured you probably hadn't eaten all day. Rose said chicken noodle soup was perfect for a cold. And she told me to tell you to get a lot of rest and drink a lot of water. She said we need you in fighting form for our battle with city hall, and made me promise to report back to her that you were taking care of yourself."

A.J. could imagine Rose issuing those instructions. What she was having a hard time imagining was that Blake had gone to all this trouble on her behalf. She looked at him quizzically. "Why did you do this?"

Blake had been asking himself the same question all the way over here. And he hadn't come up with a good answer. Or at least one he was willing to live with. "Let's just say it's Christian charity."

"I might buy that if you were a religious man."

He gave her a frustrated look. "Are you going to stand here all night, or are you going to take your temperature?"

She certainly didn't feel like standing here all night. In fact, she didn't feel like standing, period. She was starting to get light-headed again. Instead of responding, she just headed for the bathroom to retrieve the thermometer. Then she sat on the edge of the bed and stuck it in her mouth. She heard Blake rummaging in her kitchen, heard him open the microwave, heard the beeps as he programmed it. He hadn't really answered her question about why he was here. And she was too weary to try and figure it out today. But whatever the reason, she was glad he'd come.

A.J. was still sitting on the edge of the bed, thermometer in hand, when Blake appeared at her door holding a lap tray with a large glass of water and a bowl of soup.

"May I come in?"

She almost smiled. It was so like him to ask a question like that. After all, it was the conventional thing to do. "Of course. Where did you get the tray?"

"Rose had it in the back of her deli and insisted I borrow it. So what's the verdict?" He nodded toward the thermometer.

"One hundred."

He frowned. "Not good."

"It's a little better than before. The aspirin must be starting to work."

"Do you want to get back into bed? It might be easier to balance the tray."

She nodded. With an effort she scooted back and swung her legs up. A chill went through her, and she reached for the comforter.

"Are you cold?"

The man didn't miss a thing. "Chills and fever go together." She tried to keep her teeth from chattering as she spoke.

"Maybe the soup will help." He leaned down to place the tray on her lap, and as he settled it in place their gazes met. A.J. stared up into his eyes, only inches from her own, and it happened again. She wanted to reach out to him, to pull him close, to take comfort in his strong arms. The impulse scared her. She didn't want a man in her life. Not now. Not ever. She'd been down that road once. It was not a trip she wanted to take again. Especially not with this man. But she couldn't quiet the sudden staccato beat of her heart at his nearness.

Blake's gaze flickered down to the pulse beating frantically in the hollow of her throat, and when he looked back up his eyes had darkened in intensity. A.J. had a feeling that he knew exactly the effect he was having on her, and the flush on her face deepened. She tried to look away, but his compelling gaze held hers. Suddenly his eyes grew confused, and a slight frown appeared on his brow. He stood quickly, and when he spoke, his voice had an odd, appealingly husky quality. "Eat your soup."

A.J. didn't even try to speak. She just averted her gaze and picked up the spoon. When she finally ventured a glance in his direction, he was standing near the doorway watching her, his hands in his pockets, the frown still on his face.

"You ought to leave, Blake. I don't want you to get sick, too," she croaked.

"I don't get sick."

"I don't usually, either."

"Except in Afghanistan."

"That was a fluke."

"Was the leg injury a fluke, too?" The question was out before he could stop it.

Slowly she raised her gaze to his. "What leg injury?"

Too late to backtrack now. "There's nothing wrong with my eyesight, A.J. I've seen you limping."

She swallowed and averted her gaze. "That's not from Afghanistan. It's an old injury. Most of the time it doesn't bother me."

He waited, but it was clear that she wasn't going to explain further. And much as he wanted to know the story behind the injury that clearly *did* bother her on a fairly regular basis, he knew she wasn't up to discussing it today. Her eyelids were growing heavy again, and weariness was etched on her face. At least she'd eaten most of the soup. He moved toward her and lifted the tray.

"There's more soup in the fridge. And some quiche. Take it easy tomorrow, okay?"

She looked up at him, grateful he hadn't pressed her about her injury. "Thank you, Blake."

"You're welcome. Nancy and I can cover the shop on Monday if you're still not feeling well."

She nodded gratefully. "Okay."

He turned to go, pausing on the threshold to look back at her once more. A.J. stared at him, her green eyes wide and appealing. She'd lost some weight in the past week, and the fine bone structure of her face made her look almost fragile. Somewhere along the way the band that tamed her unruly curls had disappeared. Now her strawberry blond hair tumbled around her shoulders loose and soft. She looked innocent. And sweet. And very, very appealing.

A voice inside him urged him to stay.

But he was afraid.

So he listened to the other voice, the one that told him to run.

As far and as fast as he could.

A.J. took Blake up on his offer and stayed home Monday. The Board of Aldermen meeting was Tuesday, and she needed to be in top form when she made her appeal. Fortunately, when she woke on Tuesday, she felt well enough to go to work. There was just one little problem.

She had no voice.

A fact she didn't discover until she walked into Turning Leaves and tried to return Blake's greeting. She opened her mouth. She formed the words. But no sound came out. Her eyes widened in alarm.

"What's wrong?" Blake asked.

She raised her hands helplessly and pointed to her throat, then walked behind the desk and pulled out a sheet of paper. She wrote, "My voice is gone," and pushed it toward him.

He read it and frowned. "You can't talk?"

She shook her head. And suddenly felt tears welling in her eyes. Talk about rotten timing! The rest of the merchants were counting on her to make an impassioned plea tonight. She'd carefully prepared her remarks, practiced them, prepped for possible questions. What were they going to do?

Blake studied her face, his perceptive eyes missing nothing, then took her hand and led her toward the back room. He passed Nancy on the way. "Cover the front, okay?" he said over his shoulder.

When they got in the back he gently pressed A.J. into the desk chair, pulled up a chair beside her and turned on the computer. "Okay. Let's try communicating this way. You're worried about tonight, right?"

She nodded and typed, "Everyone is counting on me! What are we going to do?"

"Can't someone else speak for the group?"

Her fingers flew over the keys. "But no one else has had time to prepare. And it's a lot to dump on someone at the last minute. I could give someone my comments, but who could deliver them?"

Blake steepled his fingers, rested his elbows on the desk and stared at the computer screen. A.J. had shared the draft of her comments with him, so he knew what she planned to say. Her remarks were eloquent and touching, but also hard-hitting. No one could deliver them as well as she could. And none of the others were accustomed to standing in front of a group and making a business presentation. Except him.

Blake knew he was the logical choice to take over. He'd worked side-by-side with Jo for years, so he could talk about her commitment to the area with authority. And he'd done his homework on TIF. He understood how it worked and why the city was interested from a financial standpoint. But he also understood why using it wasn't necessarily in the best long-term interest of Maplewood.

Finally Blake turned and looked at A.J. And read in her eyes exactly what he'd just been thinking. Yet she hadn't asked him to step in. Because after meeting his parents, after the dinner in her apartment, she knew how he felt about getting publicly involved in causes.

Even one this close to his heart. And she wasn't going to pressure him.

Maybe if she had, Blake would have resisted. But because she didn't, because she had taken his feelings into consideration and refrained from asking him to put himself in an uncomfortable position, Blake felt an obligation to offer. A.J. had poured herself into this effort, as had the other merchants. He'd just attended the meetings and contributed on a peripheral level. Maybe it was time he pulled his weight.

He drew a deep breath and slowly folded his arms on the desk in front of him. "Okay. How about if I speak for the group?"

Gratitude filled her eyes, and then she turned back to the monitor and typed rapidly. "It would mean a lot to me. And to Aunt Jo, too, I know."

When their gazes met a moment later, there was a softness in A.J.'s eyes that Blake had never seen before. And suddenly he found it difficult to breathe. He cleared his throat, and scooted back slightly. "Why don't you give me your notes and I'll use them as a basis for my own comments. Can you and Nancy cover the shop part of the day while I prepare?"

She nodded. Then she laid her hand on his arm and mouthed two simple words. "Thank you."

The warmth of her touch seeped in through the oxford cloth of his shirt. And somehow worked its way to his heart.

The turnout for the meeting at city hall was better than any of the merchants had hoped. The seats were all taken twenty minutes before the proceedings were scheduled to begin, and several staff members scurried around setting up extra chairs. Even then, there wasn't enough seating. Attendees lined the walls and spilled out into the hall. By the time the meeting was called to order, the room was packed.

Routine business was dispensed with first. Then Stuart MacKenzie presented his proposal, and the floor was opened for comments and questions. A.J. glanced at Blake and gave him a thumbs-up sign. He shot her a quick grin, then stood and made his way to the microphone.

"Good evening. I'm Blake Sullivan, co-owner of Turning Leaves, a bookshop in the block that Mr. MacKenzie is targeting for his development. I represent the seven merchants on that block. I also represent Jo Williams, the original owner of Turning Leaves, who passed away a few months ago.

"I mention Jo because she was the first merchant to open a business in what twenty-some years ago was a blighted area. I'm sure some of you were around back then and remember that Maplewood wasn't exactly prime real estate. But Jo believed in the area and was convinced that with the right nurturing, it would someday rise again. The other merchants on the block felt the same way.

"Ladies and gentlemen, I don't hesitate to call these people pioneers. They courageously took a chance on an area many had written off as too far gone to be saved. They invested their time, their energy and their finances in Maplewood, and they did it with no concessions from city hall.

"Today, Maplewood is a thriving community. I submit to you that without people like the loyal, hard-working merchants in this room tonight, the incredible rebirth that this town is enjoying would never have happened. I also submit to you that one of the reasons this area is attracting new investment and renewed residential growth is because of its character, which has remained largely intact.

"Mr. MacKenzie's proposal is quite impressive. And I don't quarrel with his numbers. I'm sure the projected revenue he discussed tonight is sound. But this type of development will change the very character of Maplewood that has attracted renewed interest. Independently owned businesses, like those represented here tonight, will give way to franchises. The town will become homogenized. And in doing so, it will lose its unique appeal and charm. In the long run, I believe that will hurt, not help, the city.

"Ladies and gentlemen of the board, as you consider this proposal, I ask you to weigh the immediate financial gains against the long-term effect on this community. And I ask you to factor in the human element. Because in the end, people are what make up a town. There are good people in this room tonight. People who fight for what they believe in and work hard to make their dreams come true. And they are also people who will probably be forced to leave if this development goes through. That will be a great loss to this town. I present to you tonight signatures of more than two thousand residents who agree with this position and are against this development.

"As I said at the beginning, Jo Williams was the first to take a chance on this area. She's gone now. But her legacy lives on in the lives of the people here tonight and the businesses they have built. I hope that you don't let this legacy slip away. Thank you."

For a moment after Blake finished speaking, there was silence in the room. And then, almost as one, everyone rose and applauded wildly. But as he made his way back to his seat, Blake hardly heard the ovation or felt the hands that slapped him on the back. He just wanted to get back to A.J. Because the only reaction he really cared about was hers. He knew she'd counted on him to deliver an impassioned plea. Knew that a great deal rested on his ability to convince the board of the value the current residents added to the community.

When he reached his seat he glanced at her—and almost went limp with relief. Her face was shining, her lips tipped into a smile, telling him he'd done okay. Maybe more than okay. As he took his seat beside her, she reached over and rested her hand on his arm. And though her voice was gone, her eyes were eloquent, filled with gratitude, admiration…and something else he couldn't quite identify. But whatever it was made his throat suddenly go dry.

Only with great effort did he finally tear his gaze away and focus on the rest of the meeting. The other speakers, area residents, were also very good. The board appeared impressed, but it was hard to say what the outcome would be. Dollars spoke loudly, and in the end the board might not be able to ignore their voice. But the merchants and residents had certainly given it their best shot.

As the meeting wrapped up, A.J. nudged him and quickly jotted down a few words. He leaned over to read them. "What next?"

He wished he had a better response. "We wait."

She gave him a disgruntled look, wrote again, then turned the paper so he could read it. "And pray."

Blake studied the words. He didn't put much faith in the power of prayer himself. But he wasn't about to dissuade anyone who wanted to ask God for help.

Because it sure couldn't hurt.

Chapter Seven

"I don't feel right about leaving."

A.J. turned to Blake. "Why not? You've been planning this trip for weeks. Didn't you tell me this annual ski weekend in Colorado with your college buddies is an inviolable tradition?"

"Yeah. But you're barely back on your feet, and something could come up with the MacKenzie project."

A.J. planted her fists on her hips. "First, I'm feeling much better. Second, nothing is going to happen in the next five days with MacKenzie. The meeting was only last week. Didn't you say that your initial research showed there probably wouldn't be a decision until March or April?"

"I know, but…"

"No buts. Everyone deserves a vacation, Blake. Nancy told me you haven't taken one in over a year, other than a few long weekends. So go. Relax. Enjoy. We'll be fine."

He studied her for a moment, debating. She still looked pretty peaked to him. But he knew he'd never hear the end of it from Jack and Dave if he bailed out at the last minute. "Okay. You convinced me. But call if you need anything."

"Don't worry about us. Just have fun."

The fun part was no problem. Dave and Jack would see to that. But not worrying…that was something else entirely.

Because even though he was trying desperately to keep his business partner at arm's length, A.J. was beginning to get under his skin.

So not worrying was *not* an option.

"Hey, Jacko, what's with all the phone calls to the little woman?" Dave teased.

Jack grinned at Dave. "Don't ever let her hear you call her that. She'll deck you."

Dave chuckled. "Yeah, yeah. I know. Bonnie would do the same to me. But hey, on our annual guys' weekend, anything goes, doesn't it? What we say here stays with just the three of us. Right, Blake?"

Blake unceremoniously dumped his ski boots in the hall and grabbed a soft drink from the fridge before joining his two college buddies. "Absolutely."

Jack propped his feet on the coffee table, gazed at the crackling fire and gave a contented sigh. "Ah, this is the life."

"Yeah. But only for one long weekend a year," Dave groused good-naturedly. "Then it's back to bills and stopped-up toilets and diapers and the nine-to-five routine."

"You guys wouldn't change a thing," Blake said, dropping into one of the condo's easy chairs.

"That's true," Jack admitted, taking a long swallow of soda. "So when are you going to get with the program? I thought you'd be the first one married."

"Yeah," Dave concurred. "You were the one who wanted to settle down with the Leave-It-To-Beaver wife, raise two-point-five children and have a house with a white picket fence. What happened?"

"I've got the house," Blake said.

"So where are the two-point-five kids?"

"I think I need the wife first."

"Not these days, you don't."

"Mr. Conventional would," Jack declared with a grin.

"I didn't see either of you guys deviate from the norm," Blake pointed out.

"Guilty," Jack admitted. "So when are you going to take the plunge? Met anyone interesting lately?"

An image of A.J. flashed through his mind. In fact, she'd been on his mind a lot during the trip. As he'd maneuvered tricky moguls with expert skill, he'd thought again about her unexplained limp. And he kept picturing her when she'd been sick, looking so uncharacteristically fragile and helpless.

As the silence lengthened, Dave glanced at Jack and leaned forward with sudden interest. "I think he's been holding out on us."

Jack nodded. "Yeah. Okay, Blake, spill it. Who is she?"

Blake frowned. "Who?"

"The woman you're thinking about right now."

"What makes you think I'm thinking about a woman?"

Dave chuckled. "Because we've been there. We know the look."

"What look?"

"The I-don't-know-how-this-happened-but-I-think-I'm-falling-in-love look."

Blake's frown deepened. "You're nuts."

"Yeah? Are you going to tell me you weren't thinking about a woman just now?"

"No. I was. My partner."

Jack's eyebrows rose, and he looked at Dave. "His partner," he repeated knowingly.

Dave nodded sagely. "Sounds logical to me. My wife's my partner. How about you, Jack?"

"Yeah. Makes perfect sense."

"Come on, you guys, cut it out. I'm serious. She's my partner at the bookshop. I thought of her when you asked if I'd met any interesting women. She certainly falls into that category. But she's not my type."

Jack took a long swallow of his soft drink. "Right."

"How old is she?" Dave asked.

"I don't know. Thirtyish, I guess."

"Is she married?"

"No."

"What's her name?"

"A.J."

"Different name. What does it stand for?"

"I don't know."

"Hmm. Is she pretty?"

"Yeah."

"Do you think about her all the time?"

"No." Which was true. He didn't think about her *all* the time. Just most of the time lately. "Look, what is this? The third degree?"

"Maybe. If you won't talk, we have to ask questions," Jack said. "Like in the old days, when we first met. Man, you were a clam back then. Dave and I almost gave up on you."

"But persistence paid off," Dave interjected. "And we're not about to let you regress. So spill it."

"There's nothing to tell. Trust me, you guys will be the first to know if I ever meet the right woman."

"And this A.J. isn't it?"

"Not even close."

"Why not?"

"I told you. We're completely different. She's too unconventional and spontaneous for me. When I'm around her, I never know what to expect next. It's totally frustrating. We're at odds most of the time."

Dave glanced at Jack. "What do you think?"

Jack finished off his soft drink. "He's a goner."

Blake stared at his two best friends in the world. They grinned back at him smugly. He considered arguing the point. Then thought better of it. He'd be vindicated when nothing ever happened between him and A.J.

But for some odd reason that thought didn't give him a whole lot of satisfaction.

"What are you doing?"

The sound of Blake's voice startled A.J., and she almost lost her balance on the ladder. Blake was beside her in an instant, his hand on her arm. She turned and looked down at him, noting that he was tanned from his days of skiing. And he looked rested. Which was more than she could say for herself. They'd been exceptionally busy while he was gone, and since she wasn't back to full strength yet, the extra workload had taken a toll. Not to mention that her hip was hurting again.

"Welcome back," she said wryly.

Blake studied her face, noting her pallor and the fine lines at the corners of her eyes. She looked tired. "Are you okay?"

"Yeah, I'm fine. But don't sneak up on people like that. You scared me!" she complained.

Which was only fair, since she'd scared him. When he'd walked into the stockroom and found her wielding a heavy box while balancing on the second-highest rung of the ladder, he'd panicked.

"So what are you doing?" he repeated.

"Isn't it obvious? I'm putting a box on the shelf. Like I've done a million times since I've been here."

"I can do it for you."

She frowned. "I don't need you to. I can do it myself."

He recognized the stubborn set of her jaw, the slight tilt of her chin. She was prepared to do battle over this, but he took a different tack. "What are you trying to prove, A.J.?" he asked, his tone almost gentle.

Her eyes widened in surprise at his unexpected response. Then they grew wary. "What do you mean?"

"Why won't you let people help you?"

"I let people help me."

"When?"

She tried to think of an example. "I let you take me home the day I was sick."

"Not by choice. You'd have preferred to stick it out. If you hadn't almost keeled over, I think you would have told me to get lost. Try again." He folded his arms across his chest.

She couldn't come up with another example, so she took a defensive position. "What's your point?"

"I just want an answer to my question. What are you trying to prove by tackling a job like this when you have a bad leg and you knew I'd be back today."

"I don't have a bad leg," she said tersely. "And I wasn't trying to prove anything."

"I think you were. I think you were trying to prove that you don't need anyone, that you can handle things on your own."

"I *can* handle things on my own."

"Not all the time. And not everything. Now will you please get down off the ladder and let me put the box on the shelf?"

She glared at him. "No."

A muscle twitched in his jaw, but when he spoke his tone was mild. "Fine. Then I'll at least hold the ladder for you."

A.J. did *not* want him hanging around while she struggled with the heavy box. And she certainly didn't want him around when she descended the ladder. Climbing it hadn't been her most graceful moment. Getting down would be worse. But from the resolute look in his eyes, it was clear that Blake wasn't going anywhere. He was prepared to wait her out. So she might as well get this over with.

Gritting her teeth, A.J. turned back to the storage rack and hoisted the heavy box toward the top shelf. Much to her dismay, she missed the edge and had to make a second attempt. All the while she felt Blake's scrutiny boring into her back. Since when had he taken responsibility for her welfare? And what was with all those questions just now about trying to prove something, about not needing anyone? Why would he ask such a thing? And more importantly, why did the questions bother her?

A niggling voice in the back of her mind whispered back, "Maybe because he's hitting too close to the truth," but she shut it out. She didn't want to go there. At least not right now. Not when she still had to negotiate the rungs of the ladder.

A.J. knew her descent was awkward. And slow. And that Blake missed nothing. It took all of her willpower to turn and face him when she was at last back on level ground. She wanted to say, "See, I told you I was perfectly capable of doing this myself," but she couldn't tell such an obvious lie. She'd struggled with both the box and the ladder. And he knew it.

A.J. expected Blake to make some snide comment. But he surprised her.

"I'll put the ladder away," he said quietly.

She stepped aside without protest. His comment held no rancor, but she knew he was upset. On one level, she was touched that he cared enough to worry about her welfare. On another, she was troubled by his unsettling questions. She knew by now that Blake's instincts were generally sound and his insights keen. What had he seen in her to make him ask those questions?

A.J. didn't know the answer.

And she wasn't sure she wanted to. Because she had a feeling that it might change her life. Again. And that scared her.

Big-time.

"Well, it looks like the weather people were right for once."

A.J. looked up from the front counter and followed Nancy's gaze. Snow had begun to fall, and there was already a fine covering of white on the sidewalk.

"Seems odd for this time of year," she commented.

Nancy shrugged. "Some of our worst storms have been in early March. The good part is the snow never stays around very long."

A.J. didn't pay much attention to the weather as darkness fell. But when Nancy came back from an early dinner break, A.J. took notice of her worried expression.

"This is going to be bad," Nancy said. "The streets are already turning to ice, A.J. Maybe you should go home. You have the longest drive. Blake and I only have to go a mile or so."

A.J. walked over to the window and peered outside. Several inches of snow were already on the ground, and the streets had a slick sheen to them. She fought down a wave of panic. Ever since the accident, she'd hated driving in the snow. But there would be no way around that tonight. Even if she took Nancy's advice and left now, driving would be dangerous.

She turned back to find Blake watching her. Since their exchange in the storeroom a few days before, they'd largely avoided each other. They were polite. They were professional. But they didn't get personal. Their conversations focused on business and the weather.

She didn't have to say a word for Blake to know that she was nervous. He could feel waves of tension emanating from her body, could see the stiffness in her shoulders. He could also see the subtle, stubborn, defiant tilt of her chin as she gazed at him. So he knew his next suggestion wouldn't meet with a favorable reception. He also knew he was going to make it anyway.

"Why don't you let me drive you home?"

Before she could voice the refusal that sprang to her lips, Nancy spoke up. "That's a good idea, A.J. His car is a lot heavier than yours. It will be safer in this weather."

A.J. frowned. "But you'd be here all by yourself," she stalled.

Nancy shrugged and looked out the window. "In this weather, I doubt we'll have many customers."

"But you'll have to drive home alone, too," A.J. pointed out.

Nancy laughed. "Yeah, but I've got Bertha. She's a real heavyweight. Nothing stops her. She's solid as a rock. Besides, I don't have far to go."

A.J. thought of Nancy's older, sturdy, midsize car.

She couldn't argue that it was safer than her economy subcompact.

When A.J. finally ventured a look at Blake, he was just watching her, waiting for her decision. He hadn't argued his case, though she suspected he'd been prepared to. But Nancy had done it for him.

A.J. took one more glance out the window. The snow was coming down even harder now. She could maintain her independence and refuse Blake's offer. Or she could admit that she wasn't up to the task, use common sense and accept his help. She thought about what he'd said to her in the storeroom. She hadn't let herself dwell on it until now because it was too disturbing. But given her reaction tonight, he'd obviously been right. She did have a hard time asking for help or relying on other people. Maybe it was time to break the pattern.

Slowly A.J. turned back to Blake. "All right. Thank you."

Though Blake's casual stance didn't change, she could sense his relief in the subtle relaxing of his face muscles and the merest easing in his shoulders.

"Good. I'll go clean off the car. Give me five minutes."

By the time A.J. stepped out of the rear door of the shop, Blake was just putting away his ice scraper. He looked up when the light spilled from the doorway.

"Wait there," he called. "It's really slippery."

A.J. did as he asked. The last thing she needed was to ignore his advice and fall flat on her face. Besides, now that the ache in her hip had subsided, she didn't want to do anything that might bring it back.

Blake joined her moments later, completely covered with snow. The storm seemed to intensify with every minute that passed. "Take my arm and hold on. This lot is like a skating rink."

Again she didn't argue. Slowly they made their way to his car, and even before they were halfway there, A.J. knew she had made a wise decision in accepting his offer. She could barely walk on the slippery surface, and driving would be a nightmare. Just riding in a car would be bad enough.

Blake helped her into the passenger seat, then came around to his side and brushed himself off before sliding behind the wheel. He looked over at A.J. Snowflakes still clung to her strawberry blond curls, and he smiled. "You look like you have stars in your hair," he said.

She tried to smile. "Better than in my eyes, I suppose."

He focused on those green eyes for a moment. No stars there. Instead he saw fear. He watched as she swallowed convulsively, then nervously brushed back a stray strand of hair with shaking fingers. She was absolutely terrified, he realized with a start. Not just a little nervous about driving in bad weather. But terrified. This time he followed his instincts. He reached for her hand and gave it a squeeze.

"Hey, it will be okay. I'll get you home safely," he said gently.

For a moment she seemed surprised by his action. But she didn't pull away. Again, she valiantly tried to smile. And failed. "I just don't like driving in snow," she said.

There was more to her terror than that. He wanted to ask what it was, but didn't. This wasn't the time. "Just relax. You'll be home before you know it."

But he was wrong. It took them ten minutes just to go six blocks, slipping and sliding the whole way. It was so bad that even Blake, who never minded driving in bad weather, was getting worried. When they skidded dangerously close to a parked car as he maneuvered one corner, he pulled to the side and turned to A.J. She hadn't said one word since they'd left, and he'd been so busy trying to navigate that he hadn't looked at her. But now he realized that she had a death grip on the dashboard, and in the light from the street lamp he could see that the color had drained from her face.

"This isn't looking good, A.J." When she didn't respond, he reached over and laid a hand on her arm. He could feel the tremors running through her body. "A.J.?"

With an effort she tore her gaze away from the street and stared at him, her eyes wide. "Wh-what?"

"I said this isn't looking good."

"I kn-know." The catch in her voice spoke eloquently of her fear.

"Look, I don't think we should try to make it to your apartment. I have a guest room, and I'm only half a mile from here. Would you consider staying there tonight?"

"At your place? You mean…just us?"

"I'll sleep next door. My elderly neighbors are on a cruise and they gave me a key to their house."

"I don't want to put you out of your own home."

"It's not a problem, A.J. They have a huge couch in the family room. I'll be fine for one night."

She took a deep breath and slowly nodded. "Okay."

"Good. Hang in there. It shouldn't take us long to get to my place."

By the time Blake pulled into his attached garage twenty minutes later, even he was tense. He'd driven in some pretty bad weather, but the icy conditions he'd just encountered ranked right up there with a raging blizzard he, Dave and Jack had once encountered on a drive back to the Denver airport from one of their annual ski trips.

"Sit tight. I'll get your door," he told A.J.

A moment later, he pulled it open. When she didn't move, he leaned down. "A.J.?"

She was still staring straight ahead, gripping the dashboard, and he could tell that a single tear had slipped from her eye and left a trail halfway down her cheek. He leaned in and gently touched her shoulder. "It's okay. We're home. Everything's fine," he said soothingly. "Come on, I'll help you out."

Automatically she swung her legs out of the car. When she faced him her eyes were slightly glazed and she seemed almost to be in shock. He took her hands and urged her out of the car, shutting the door with his hip. And then, for the second time that night, he followed his instincts and pulled her into his arms.

A.J. didn't protest. In fact, she went willingly, letting him wrap his arms around her and hold her close. She laid her head on his shoulder, and her own arms went around him. He could feel her trembling, and he stroked her back with one hand, letting the other move up to cradle her head.

"Everything's okay. You're safe," he murmured softly near her ear.

A.J. knew she should step out of Blake's embrace. Knew that her acquiescence was completely out of character and that he would eventually want an explanation. But she couldn't help herself. As she'd stared out the window of the car on the drive to his house, watching the snowflakes beat against the glass, her nightmarish memories had replayed themselves in her mind for the second time in a couple of weeks. Once again, their vividness had taken her breath away. Even now her heart was pounding and her breathing was erratic. She needed something solid and sure to cling to. Namely, Blake. In his arms, she felt safe and protected. It was an illusion, of course. She knew that. But it felt good. And for just a moment, she let herself pretend that it was true.

A.J. wasn't sure how long she remained in Blake's embrace. But finally, when her trembling subsided, she took a long, shuddering breath and made a move to disengage. He let her step back, but continued to hold her upper arms as he searched her face in the dim light of the garage. She was still pale, and the freckles across the bridge of her nose were more pronounced than usual.

"A.J.?"

"I—I'm okay, Blake. Sorry about this. Storms freak me out."

There was a brief hesitation before he spoke. "Okay. Let's get inside where it's warm."

He kept his arm protectively on the small of her

back as he fitted the key in the lock. When the door swung open, he ushered her into a small mud room.

"Let me take your coat."

He helped her take it off, then shrugged out of his own and hung both on hooks. "I'll show you the guest room and let you settle in while I get a fire going."

He led the way through a cozy kitchen/breakfast room combo, across a small entry foyer and down a hall to a door near the end.

"This is really part office, part den," he apologized as they stepped into the room. It was furnished with a modular desk and computer, and a couch stood against one wall. "The sofa is a sleeper. It's not the most comfortable bed around, but it works pretty well for emergencies."

"This will be fine for one night, Blake."

When he spoke, it was almost like he hadn't heard her. "I'll tell you what. Why don't you take my room tonight? It has a real bed, and it would be better than…"

"I'm perfectly fine with the sofa sleeper," she interrupted.

He could tell from the stubborn tilt of her chin that arguing wasn't going to get him anywhere. So he decided to save his persuasive powers for other discussions. Like finding out why she was so terrified of snowstorms. And why she sometimes limped.

"Okay." He walked over to the sofa, quickly dispensed with the cushions, and in one lithe movement pulled the bed open. "There are blankets in the closet in here," he said, nodding toward the other side of the room. "And I have extra sheets in the hall closet."

She followed him into the hall, reaching for the bedding as he withdrew it. "I can handle this. I'd rather you spend your time getting that fire going," she said.

He handed them over without resistance. "The bathroom's right across the hall," he told her, nodding toward an adjacent doorway. "There are fresh towels under the sink. There's also an extra toothbrush under there."

She gave him a small smile. "I see you're always prepared for guests."

He looked at her, and paused for a moment as if debating his next words. "No one's ever spent the night here before," he told her quietly.

Her grin faded. A.J. had been joking. Blake wasn't. He was telling her in no uncertain terms that he didn't have overnight guests. And that he didn't believe in casual intimacy.

A.J. had no idea how to respond to this revelation. So she didn't. "Well, I—I guess I'll go make up the bed," she stammered.

And before he could respond, she headed for the den.

Blake watched her go. Now why had he told her that? The statement had been true enough. He didn't believe in one-night stands or living together. When he met the right woman, he would make a commitment to her. Publicly. Formally. That was the only way intimacy had any meaning. And for some reason he'd wanted A.J. to know that. He wasn't sure why. But tonight wasn't the time to figure it out. Not when he had a fire to make and a dinner to prepare.

As A.J. made the bed and freshened up, she thought

about Blake's comment. It was something you might say to a woman you were interested in having a relationship with. But they were just business partners. Maybe her receptiveness to his embrace in the garage had prompted the disclosure. But there had been nothing intimate in his touch. She had felt only caring and comfort and friendship. So she didn't think that was why he'd said it. There was something more. But tonight wasn't the time to figure it out. Her nerves were already shot from the drive here. They couldn't take much more.

She opened the closet and spotted the blankets. But her attention was diverted by trophies that shared space on the same shelf. Curiously, she stood on tiptoe to read the inscriptions. There were several for running and biking events, and even one for a very good finish in a triathlon. All were of fairly recent vintage. She stared at them, impressed. She'd known Blake was in good shape, known that he was a runner and cyclist. Nancy had mentioned it. But she'd thought his interest was purely recreational. She'd had no idea he was competitive in either sport. Or that he was a swimmer.

Thoughtfully she withdrew a blanket, and as she turned back toward the sofa she noticed a couple of framed certificates near the desk. On impulse, she moved closer to examine them. One was an acknowledgment of Blake's work with a local homeless shelter. The other recognized his contributions as a board member to the Big Brothers organization. Her glance fell on the three-month calendar under a clear mat on his desk, and her gaze was drawn to the Saturday she'd been so ill, when he'd refused to sub for her at the shop. There were meetings listed for both organizations.

A.J. took a deep breath. She'd learned more about Blake in the past few minutes than she had since they'd met. In the garage, she'd learned just how caring and compassionate he was. She'd learned he had strong moral principles when it came to relationships. That he was a superb and disciplined athlete. And that he believed in helping those less fortunate. His choice of organizations to support was also clearly a reflection of his own upbringing.

When they'd met, A.J. had written Blake off as a stuffy, inflexible, stick-in-the-mud loner. But as she was beginning to discover, there was a whole lot more to this complex man than met the eye. He might not be the most spontaneous guy in the world, but there were some very good reasons for that. And he was able to bend when necessary. His willingness to step in and speak in her place at the Board of Aldermen meeting was clear evidence of that. And also of his kindness and compassion. She knew he hated confrontation and anything that reeked of protest. But he'd put himself front and center in that situation anyway. For her, and for their cause. And she deeply admired—and respected—him for that.

As A.J. thoughtfully made her way to the kitchen, she peeked into a darkened room as she passed. It was empty except for a weight set and a racing bike. More evidence of his training regime. He skied, too. It was telling that all of his sports were solitary, she reflected.

When she got to the kitchen, she found him chopping onions. "What can I do to help?"

He turned toward her. Her face had more color now and the tension had eased. "Why don't you just go in and enjoy the fire?" he said with a relieved smile.

"I'd like to help."

"I think I have everything under control. But I'm not doing anything as exotic as the meal you made. Just meat loaf and mashed potatoes. I hope that's okay."

"I eat normal food, too," she teased. "If you have some fresh vegetables, I could make a stir-fry. And I could probably put together a salad if you have some lettuce."

He nodded toward the refrigerator. "Help yourself to anything you can find."

A.J. peered into the refrigerator and rummaged around a bit. "There's plenty of stuff here for both," she said, her voice slightly muffled. She began withdrawing items and set them on the counter beside Blake. "Where are your spices?"

He reached past her and pulled open a cabinet, his rolled-up sleeve brushing her face. She couldn't help but notice the sprinkling of dark hair on his forearm. Or the subtle masculine scent that invaded her nostrils. Her pulse suddenly tripped into double time, and she drew a sharp breath.

Blake looked at her. "Are you okay?"

She forced herself to nod, but that was a lie. She hadn't had such a visceral reaction to a man since Eric. And she'd forgotten how to deal with it. So she focused her attention on the spice rack. "Do you have a paring knife?" she asked when she could finally speak.

He rinsed off the one he'd been using and handed it to her. "Ask and you shall receive."

She smiled. "Don't tell me you're quoting the Bible!"

He shrugged. "I have a passing acquaintance with some of the more common scripture passages. One of my college roommates was a pretty devout Christian, so I learned a few things from him. He even dragged me to services a few times."

"I take it you weren't impressed."

"Not enough to go on my own."

"Hmm. I guess it's different if you aren't raised in a Christian environment. My faith has always been so much a part of my life…it's gotten me through some tough times."

"Such as?"

A.J.'s hand stilled for a moment. "Well, the deaths of my parents, for starters," she said quietly. "My dad died of a heart attack when I was eleven. My mom died four years ago. Even though I still miss them terribly, it's a great comfort to know that they're in a better place. My sorrow when they died was for me, not them."

"But how do you reconcile a good and loving God with what you witnessed in Afghanistan? The hardship and deprivation and violence and starvation?"

"I guess that's what faith is all about. It's accepting the things we don't understand, knowing that God does. And He gave us free will. A lot of the bad things that happen in the world are because people make wrong choices, and then innocent people suffer. That's not His choice. It's ours."

"What about natural disasters, like floods and earthquakes? Those aren't caused by human choices, and thousands of innocent people are hurt."

"I don't know the answer to that, Blake. Only God does. And I wouldn't presume to try and understand the mind of God. It's far beyond our human capacity. It all comes down again to faith. But you only have to read the salvation story to know how deeply God cares for all of us. He gave us His own son. And He suffered, too, while in human form. Suffering is part of life."

Blake slid the meat loaf into the oven. "That's probably the best explanation I've ever heard to those questions," he said, turning to face her.

She shook her head. "Then you haven't been talking to the right people. I can't give you a lot of theology. I can only tell you what's in my heart. But if you're ever interested in learning more, the minister at my new church is wonderful. I'd be happy to introduce you."

"I'll keep that in mind. Shall we sit by the fire while the meat loaf cooks?"

"Sure."

"Go ahead, and I'll join you in a minute."

A.J. made her way into the living room. The decor was conservative, but comfortable, which didn't surprise her. The only unexpected thing in the room was a crudely carved folk-art statue on the coffee table. It was of a small boy, running exuberantly, his hands joyously stretched toward the sky. The child's expression reflected absolute contentment and happiness, and perfectly captured what childhood should be all about. A.J. recognized it immediately. It was from the Good Samaritan collection at the shop. She knew it had sold, but she didn't know who had bought it. She wondered if Blake saw, in the carving, all that he'd missed in his own childhood.

When he joined her a moment later, he was carrying two crystal goblets of sparkling cider.

"Fancy," she said. "Looks like a special occasion."

"Maybe it is."

She glanced into his warm, caring eyes, and suddenly found it difficult to swallow. Tonight had been special in many ways. She'd learned a great deal about the man across from her. She'd recognized that at some point she'd have to deal with the questions he'd raised about her unwillingness to rely on other people. She'd realized that the romantic part of her heart hadn't died with Eric, after all. And she was now facing a whole evening alone with the man who had reawakened those feelings in her. Feelings she wasn't yet ready to face. Not with any man. And certainly not with this man.

But as she gazed at him, she was forced to acknowledge that, ready or not, she would have to deal with those feelings soon.

And as Blake handed her a glass, then sat beside her, she realized that the storm raging outside couldn't hold a candle to the storm that was suddenly raging in her heart.

Chapter Eight

"That was a wonderful meal, Blake." A.J. dipped a tea bag in a cup of hot water as she spoke. "How did you learn to make such great meat loaf?"

"After I'd been working a couple of years, I got pretty tired of fast food and frozen dinners. So I bought a beginners' cookbook, and I actually learned a lot. Nothing to compare with that couscous dish you made, though."

She shrugged his compliment aside. "It's not hard. The people in Afghanistan have learned to prepare simple meals with inexpensive ingredients. It's the spices that make the difference. The dish I served your parents is one of my favorites."

"I can see why. Shall we go back in by the fire?"

"Sure." A.J. stood and moved toward the living room, pausing to gaze out the window as she cradled her mug in her hands. "It still looks terrible out."

She felt Blake come up behind her to look over her

shoulder. His breath was warm on her ear, and her own breathing seemed to speed up. She half expected him to put his hands on her shoulders. It would somehow have seemed natural. But he didn't.

"I doubt this is going to stop anytime soon. It's a good thing we didn't try to make it to your place."

She felt him move away, and when her breathing was more or less under control, she turned and made her way back toward the fire. Blake was sitting on the couch, one arm casually draped across the back, an ankle crossed over a knee. He was sipping a cup of coffee, and looked completely relaxed. And oblivious to her unexpected reaction to his nearness. She considered sitting in the chair next to the fire instead of joining him on the couch, figuring that if she put a little distance between them her nerves might settle down. But she also figured that might raise questions. After all, her reaction appeared to be entirely one-sided. Blake had been nothing more than friendly all evening. Even the earlier embrace that had played havoc with her emotions seemed to have left him completely unaffected. It was her own reactions she had to worry about. Not his.

She sat beside him, careful to keep a respectable distance between them, but not so much that it would seem odd.

"How's the tea?" he asked.

"Comforting. Especially on a cold night."

"My mother always liked tea."

"How are your parents doing?"

"Fine, I guess."

"I take it communication is sporadic, at best."

"Yeah."

"That's too bad, Blake."

He shrugged. "That's how it's always been since I left home."

"You could change that."

"Meaning you think I should?"

She lifted one shoulder in response. "You have to make that decision for yourself. I'm just suggesting that I think they'd be receptive."

As usual, A.J.'s instincts were accurate. Blake knew his parents would welcome a reconciliation. They'd made overtures through the years, which he had ignored. The ball was in his court. And lately, he'd been toying with the notion of initiating some contact. He just wasn't sure how to begin after all these years.

"It's not that easy to start over," he said quietly, studying his coffee.

She was silent for so long that he finally looked over at her. She was gazing into the fire, and there was such raw pain in her eyes that his throat constricted with tenderness.

"What are you thinking?" he asked, his voice a shade deeper than usual.

With an effort, she pulled her gaze from the flames and looked at him. "I was thinking about what you said. I agree. Starting over is never easy. But it can be done."

He took a sip of his coffee. His impulse was to reach out and take her hand again. But he'd done enough of that for one night. He was about to ask some pretty personal questions, and he didn't want to scare her off.

"You sound like you've had experience at that," he said carefully.

She turned away, and he saw her swallow convulsively. For a moment he thought she wasn't going to answer. But finally she spoke, her voice so low it was almost a whisper. "Yeah."

He waited a beat. "Is it something you want to talk about?"

A.J. drew an unsteady breath, then turned back to him. There was nothing but kindness and compassion in his eyes. He wasn't pushing her to confide, but it was clear that he was willing to offer a sympathetic ear. She didn't share her trauma with many people. It was part of her philosophy of putting the past behind her and making the most of today. But for some reason, she wanted to tell this man her story.

"I haven't told a lot of people," she ventured, her voice tentative.

"I'm a good listener. And you certainly have a captive audience tonight," he said, flashing her an encouraging smile.

A.J. took a deep breath. Blake had shared with her some of his issues with his parents. It seemed only right that she share some of her past with him. And he seemed genuinely interested. "Did Aunt Jo ever tell you much about me?"

"No. Family was a painful subject for me. She mentioned her great-nieces a few times, but to be honest, I never encouraged her to talk about you or your sisters."

"That's what I thought. If you'd known about the ac-

cident, you probably would have put two and two together and figured out why I sometimes limp."

He set his mug on the table and angled his body toward her. "So the accident has nothing to do with
Afghanistan?"

"Only indirectly. It was one of the reasons I decided
to go." She tightened her grip on her mug and stared
into the fire. "It's so hard to know where to start."

"The beginning is always a good place."

She tried to smile, but couldn't quite pull it off. "We
could be here all night."

"I'm not planning to go far, anyway."

"Okay. Then I'll give you the condensed version of
the A. J. Williams life story."

"Start with the A.J."

She frowned at him. "What do you mean?"

"What do the initials stand for?"

"Oh." She made a face. "Abigail Jeanette."

"Pretty."

"Not for a tomboy. Abigail Jeanette is such an old-
fashioned, ladylike name. I was always tall and lanky
and athletic. It didn't fit. So I shortened it to A.J. early
on."

Blake didn't agree with A.J.'s assessment of her fem-
inine charms, but he let her comment pass for the moment.

"Anyway, thanks to my mom and dad, I was totally
comfortable with who I was. They always encouraged
me to do my best, and I did. I excelled at basketball and
soccer, and I also did well academically. Frankly, I intimidated a lot of the guys in high school because I

could compete with them pretty much on their own terms and often come out the winner. Which was okay, because they respected me and considered me one of the guys. But on the other hand, when it came to dating, I wasn't even a contender. Besides, I was taller than a lot of them. So they just didn't think of me in those terms.

"Because of that, I didn't date in high school. Since I couldn't do anything about my height, and I wasn't about to play the coy, incompetent, demure type just to get men interested in me, I figured dates in the future would be few and far between, too. Not many guys have egos strong enough to handle an extremely independent woman.

"So I focused on preparing for a career that would provide a comfortable living. Since I'd always been good with numbers, I majored in business and then got into an M.B.A. program. That's where I met Eric. He was in his last year when I started."

A.J. paused to swallow painfully, and Blake leaned closer. He'd never heard her mention that name before. But the man had obviously been important to her. He found himself wondering who Eric was, and if he'd hurt her.

"We dated for a year and a half, while I was working on my M.B.A.," A.J. continued. "And when he asked me to marry him, I thought I could never be any happier. We decided to go on a ski trip with a church group over spring break to celebrate. We had a great time, and we made some wonderful plans for our future. I'll remember that trip as long as I live."

A.J. paused, and Blake saw her swallow. He knew she was getting to the traumatic part of the story, and he wanted to reach out to her. But he held back, knowing she was not yet ready for his comfort. When she spoke again, her voice was flat and lifeless.

"The...the accident happened on the way back. A couple of hours after we left the resort. I remember that it was quiet on the bus. We were all tired, and a lot of people were drifting off to sleep. I had my head on Eric's shoulder, and I had this wonderful feeling of deep contentment and happiness. It was pitch-dark outside the windows of the bus, and huge snowflakes were beating against the glass. But I felt insulated from the storm—warm and protected and safe."

She drew a ragged breath and reached up with shaking fingers to brush a stray wisp of hair off her forehead. Her gaze was fixed on the fire, but it was clear that she was seeing something else entirely, something far away and long ago.

"M-my memories after that are sketchy. I heard the brakes slam. And there was a sudden jarring, like the bus was trying to stop. There was an odd sideways motion. And then...the world tilted. People screamed. I grabbed onto Eric, and he reached for me. W-we looked at each other, and I remember the fear and...and the panic in his eyes. And then e-everything went black."

A single tear slid down her cheek, and a sob caught in her throat. "I f-found out later that our bus slid off the road. We went over an embankment. A lot of people were killed...including Eric."

Blake sucked in a sharp breath, and she turned to

him. Her eyes were dull with pain, her voice mechanical now, almost clinical. "I survived, but my hip was crushed. It took three operations to restore a semblance of normalcy and two long years of therapy before I could walk properly. During that time I reevaluated my career plans. I'd lost interest in the business world. It just seemed so meaningless. I felt a need to do something more important with my life. That's when I discovered Good Samaritan. You know the rest."

Blake stared at the woman beside him, his face a mask of shock. So many things made sense now. Her independent spirit, forged from hardship. Her limp, not only a permanent physical impairment but a constant reminder of the tragedy that had stolen her fiancé and turned her world upside down. Her fear of driving in snow. And perhaps her vagabond lifestyle. Jo had hinted as much in her letter to him. Had suggested that even A.J. didn't fully understand why she'd never put down roots since the accident. But suddenly Blake did. If you'd made plans and prepared for a certain kind of life, only to have it snatched away, who wouldn't be afraid to make those kinds of plans, those commitments, again? Many people wouldn't survive the kind of loss A.J. had suffered even one time; twice would be unthinkable. In her mind, it probably wasn't worth the risk.

Another tear slid silently down A.J.'s cheek, and Blake's gut clenched painfully. Gently he reached over and pried the mug out of her fingers. They were ice cold, as was her tea. He set the mug on the coffee table and then turned back to her. She looked fragile. And haunted. And so alone.

He'd refrained from touching her before. He didn't now. Without stopping to consider the consequences, he closed the distance between them and pulled her into his arms, cradling her slender body against his solid chest. He could feel the rapid thudding of her heart, could hear her uneven breathing. For a moment she went rigid, and he was afraid she'd pull back. But then she relaxed against him, and he heard a stifled sob as she buried her face in his neck.

"It's okay, A.J. I'm here. Just hold on to me," he said unevenly, his voice tattered at the edges. He felt the tremors run through her, felt the evidence of her silent tears in the erratic rise and fall of her chest. And as he stroked her back, it suddenly occurred to him that in light of all she'd been through—the pain and suffering and loss—his own childhood trauma seemed petty. If she could rebuild her life out of the ashes, surely he could find a way to reconnect with his parents. To put the ghosts of his childhood to rest once and for all.

He held her for a long time, and gradually he felt her sobs subside. But she didn't move out of his arms immediately. And he was in no hurry to let her go.

Finally, though, she drew a deep breath and pushed back. When she looked at him, her face was flushed and she seemed embarrassed. "Sorry about that."

"About sharing your story?"

"No. Sorry I fell apart."

"You're entitled."

She sniffled, and he reached into his pocket and held out a handkerchief. "I always have a spare," he told her when she hesitated.

A ghost of a smile flickered across her face. "You would."

"Is that an insult?"

"No. I'm beginning to appreciate your ability to always be prepared." And other qualities as well, she acknowledged silently.

He reached over and traced the course of a tear down her cheek. She went absolutely still at his touch. "A.J., I'm so sorry."

He didn't need to say any more. She could see the depth of compassion in his eyes. "Thanks. It w-was a really hard time."

"How did you make it through?"

"My mom was still alive then, and she was incredibly supportive. So were my sisters. That's why I think it's so important to make sure family ties are strong. My faith helped sustain me, too. Those were the reasons I survived."

"I think there might have been a dash of fortitude and determination thrown in, too. Not to mention discipline and strength."

She shrugged. "Those things alone wouldn't have gotten me through without my family and my faith."

Suddenly she yawned, and Blake glanced at his watch. "It's getting late. And you've had a long and emotionally draining day. Why don't you make it an early night?"

"I want to help with the dishes first."

"Not tonight."

"But it's not fair to…"

"Not tonight," he interrupted, this time more firmly.

"I know you're used to doing things for yourself. After hearing your story, I understand why that's so important to you. I also understand something else." He paused, and his gaze held hers. When he spoke again, his voice was gentle. "Did it ever occur to you that maybe one of the reasons you don't like to let people help you is because you don't want to begin to rely on someone again who might not be around tomorrow? That maybe you're afraid to make plans for a future that might not come to pass?"

She stared at him, momentarily speechless. Was she afraid? Not only of letting people help, but of settling down, putting down roots, making plans? But fear wouldn't be consistent with her faith. She believed in relying on God, of putting her trust in Him. So she couldn't be afraid. That had nothing to do with being independent, of taking care of herself. And as for not making plans or putting down roots, well, that was easily explained. She simply didn't want to be tied down by material things or commitments that could make her less open and available to God's call.

Those explanations had always worked for her before. Yet forced to examine her motivations under Blake's discerning eye, they suddenly didn't seem to ring quite true. But she didn't want to deal with that tonight. So she ignored his questions.

"Okay. I'll go to bed." Eager to escape both the man and the doubts he'd raised, she stood abruptly. Too abruptly. Because she momentarily lost her balance.

Blake was on his feet instantly, his grip firm and sure on her arms, steadying her. What A.J. saw in his eyes made her heart stop, then race on. Concern. Compassion. Respect. And something more. Something powerful and compelling. Something she wasn't yet ready to deal with. She needed to put some distance between them. Quickly. But she seemed unable to move.

Blake stared at the woman who was mere inches away, their eyes almost level. Her story had resonated deeply with him, touched a place in his heart that had never been touched before. He'd known A.J. was a good person with a kind heart. He'd learned, over time, that she was smart and savvy and had great instincts. He'd also known she was strong. But until tonight, he hadn't known just how strong.

In the past, he'd used the word interesting to describe her. That term still fit. But so did intriguing. And absorbing. And exciting. Not to mention appealing. Very appealing. Too appealing.

Blake had been attracted to other women. More than a few, in fact. Something about each of them had caught his fancy, made his pulse accelerate. The difference with A.J. was that *everything* about her was beginning to make his pulse race. He liked her spunk. He liked her spirit. He liked her kindness and compassion and intellect. He liked that she challenged him to think differently, to take some risks, to reevaluate long-held opinions. She kept him on his toes. She made him smile. On top of everything else, she was beautiful. And he was having a harder and harder time imagining his life without her.

That scared him. But not enough to suppress the yearning that sprang to life as he stared into her eyes.

Only the faint crackle of the fire broke the stillness in the room, and he felt a warmth that didn't come from the dying embers in the fireplace a few feet away. Suddenly he longed to run his fingers through her soft hair. To hold her close, so close that she forgot the past and the future and became lost in the moment.

But this wasn't the time. She was too vulnerable. And things could get out of hand. He already had enough regrets in his life. He didn't want to add one more.

With a supreme effort, he released her arms, stepped back and shoved his fists into his pockets. "Sleep well," he said huskily. "I'll lock the door behind me when I go next door."

Her only response was a jerky nod. And then she fled.

Blake watched her go. And when he reached for their mugs a moment later, he discovered that his own hands were trembling.

He stared at them and frowned. There could be a number of explanations for his reaction. But in his heart, he knew that fear was the primary culprit. Because Jack's words in Colorado now seemed prophetic. Maybe he *was* a goner. Which was not good. Because despite all her good qualities, logic told him that A.J. wasn't his type at all.

But his heart wasn't listening.

The fragrant aroma of freshly brewed coffee greeted Blake when he stepped inside the front door of his house the next morning, and he made a beeline for the kitchen. Obviously A.J. was up already. He certainly hoped she'd slept better than he had. By the time he'd finally drifted off, after tossing and turning for hours on his neighbor's uncomfortable couch, it had been close to three o'clock in the morning. Right now he needed a shot of caffeine.

He saw she wasn't in the kitchen, so Blake poured himself a cup of strong, black coffee and headed for the bathroom to shower. Normally he slept in on Sunday, then ran or biked for a couple of hours, followed by a swim at the nearby gym. However, given the storm, he doubted he'd be going anywhere today. Except to take A.J. back to the shop to get her car. And he was in no hurry to do that. He was looking forward to a leisurely morning with his unexpected houseguest

When he emerged from the bathroom a few minutes later, he sniffed appreciatively and followed his nose to the kitchen. A.J. was at the stove now, intent on turning what appeared to be a fluffy omelet, her lower lip caught in her teeth, a slight frown marring her brow. Her focus was absolute, her concentration intense. Blake's gaze flickered to the table. Two places were set—a first for him at breakfast. He was used to grabbing an energy bar or stopping to pick up a bagel somewhere. He definitely preferred this.

He waited until she'd successfully flipped the omelet before he spoke, in a voice that was still slightly roughened by sleep. "Good morning."

She turned abruptly, then felt her face grow warm. She'd never seen Blake in such casual attire. Worn jeans outlined his muscular legs, and a T-shirt hugged his broad chest and revealed impressive biceps. His damp hair was slicked back, and as he stood there, one shoulder propped against the door frame, his hands in his pockets, her pulse began to race. She'd struggled late into the night trying to get her emotions under control. And thought she'd succeeded. But one look at Blake disproved that theory.

She turned back to the stove and made a pretense of checking the omelet. "Yes, it is. The road crews have been through, and the sun is shining. We're no longer marooned," she said brightly.

Blake didn't think that was particularly good news, but he'd come to the same conclusion himself as he walked home from his neighbor's house. Driving would be manageable today, except on secondary roads.

"Breakfast is ready," A.J. said over her shoulder.

He waited until she'd deposited their plates on the table, then held her chair for her. When she looked surprised, he gave her an endearing grin. "Mr. Conventional. Sorry," he said.

She smiled. "You don't have to apologize. A lot of conventions are nice."

"This looks great, A.J. You didn't have to go to all this trouble." He helped himself to some toast.

"It wasn't any trouble. I don't bother much with breakfast during the week, but I try to do something a little nicer on Sundays. I usually eat it alone, though, so I have to admit the conversation is much better today."

He chuckled, a pleasing sound that rumbled deep in his chest. "So what else do you do on Sundays?"

"Go to church." She glanced regretfully at her watch.

"But I don't see how I can make it today. The last service is at ten. By the time you drop me at the shop to pick up my car, timing will be pretty tight."

"Would you like me to take you?"

A.J.'s hand froze, her fork halfway to her mouth, astonishment written on her face. But she didn't look any more surprised than he felt. Where in the world had that come from? He hadn't been inside a church in years.

"You mean drop me off? Or stay?" she asked cautiously.

She'd given him an out. He could just leave her at the door and come back for her later. But for some reason, he hated this interlude with A.J. to end. If going to church would buy him another hour or two with her, it would be worth the sacrifice. Besides, he still needed to sort through his feelings about his houseguest, and maybe a visit to church would help him do that. Churches were supposed to be good places to think, weren't they?

"I could stay."

A.J. stared at him. "Why?"

He felt his neck grow warm. "Why not?"

"I don't know. It's just that…well, you told me you didn't really practice any religion. I'm just…surprised. But of course, you're welcome to come with me. Our minister is great. You might even enjoy it."

He doubted that. But he had to admit he was a little intrigued. First his parents had told him they were attending church. They were the two most unlikely candidates he could think of to practice organized religion. Yet when they'd spoken about it briefly during dinner at A.J.'s, he'd seen a look in their eyes that told him they'd found something special. And there was no question that A.J.'s faith was the foundation of her life. It had seen her through some tough times, given her stability and security when everything else in her world had fallen apart.

If Christianity was powerful enough to win over his parents, and to sustain A.J. through all of her trials and tribulations, maybe it was worth exploring.

Brad Matthews was a great speaker. No question about it.

Blake hadn't really planned to listen to the sermon during the service. He'd figured that would be a good time to mull over the situation with A.J. But the minister at her church had grabbed him with his opening line and never let him go. The man spoke in simple, but compelling, terms. And oddly enough, his message seemed to be directed at Blake. He'd used the story of the prodigal son as the basis for his sermon, and talked about the difficulties—and importance—of reconciliation. And his concluding words really struck home.

"As we leave this place of worship and return to our daily lives, it's easy to leave the Lord's message behind, too. But that's not what He wants us to do. He wants us to take His words and apply them to our lives. To live the words He spoke, not just read them on Sunday.

"The story of the prodigal son is about a young man who made mistakes. Who left his family behind, cut off all contact, and isolated himself from the people who loved him the most. Yet his father welcomed him back.

The parallel between this story and our relationship with God is obvious. But there are lessons we can apply in our own human relationships as well. It doesn't matter who the wronged party is. It doesn't matter who left and who stayed behind. It doesn't matter if it's a parent, a spouse, a child or a friend who is estranged. All that matters is that someone take the first step to mend the rift. And that the other person be receptive.

"If there are relationships in your life that need mending, remember the lessons of the prodigal son. It requires courage to take the first step, to initiate a reconciliation. Because it usually means we have to admit we've been wrong. Or that we have to forgive someone. Pride is a fault we all share, and it often gets in the way of reconciliation, whether we're the wronged party or the one who did wrong. On our own, we may not be able to overcome the hurdles that stand in the way of mending fences with those we love. But God can help. Call on Him. He's waiting for you. And with Him by your side, all things are possible.

"Now, let us pray…"

The congregation rose, and Blake followed suit. As he did so, he saw Nancy and Eileen a few rows away. His gaze connected with Nancy's as she turned to say something to her daughter, and the look of surprise on her face was almost comical. Her mouth actually dropped open. Blake nodded, but even after he looked back to the minister, he knew she was still staring at him.

He couldn't blame her. She'd tried a number of times to convince him to attend services with her. He'd always adamantly refused. So he knew he'd have some explaining to do tomorrow.

Of course, his presence at church would be easy enough to justify in light of the snowstorm. He could just say that A.J. seemed disturbed about missing the service, and he'd volunteered to take her. Nancy would probably buy that.

But it would be harder to explain if he came again.

And that's exactly what he was thinking about doing.

Strange. His attendance today had been prompted by a desire to spend more time with A.J. But that wasn't why he was considering returning. It was more fundamental than that.

The fact was, for some odd reason, sitting in the church today, listening to the music and hearing the word of God spoken and discussed, he felt almost as if he'd come home. And for the first time in a long while, he'd felt at peace.

Blake didn't understand why he'd experienced those feelings. But he wanted to.

And he figured this was the place to find the answers.

Chapter Nine

The bell jangled over the front door of the bookshop, and A.J. and Blake simultaneously looked up. George was bearing down on them, still wearing his white apron. And he looked upset. A.J. glanced at Blake, then turned toward the older man.

"What's wrong, George?" she asked.

"I hear something today that is not good," he said, huffing as he tried to catch his breath.

"Let's go in the back," Blake suggested. He signaled to Nancy, and she relieved them at the front desk.

George followed them, and Blake waved him to a chair. "What's up?"

George wiped his hands nervously on his apron. "I hear a patron talking about MacKenzie and the development. So I stayed close by and listened. He said that the city is going to use the TIF after all."

Blake frowned. "Do you know who this man is, George?"

"No. I never see him before. But he had on what you call a…power suit. Expensive. He sounded like he knew what he was talking about."

A.J. gave Blake a worried look. "What do you think?"

"I think I better talk to my neighbor and see what I can find out."

"You will do that soon?" George asked.

"Tonight."

"And you will let us know what you find?"

"Of course. Let's not panic until we get some solid information. Maybe the man you heard was just speculating and nothing has actually happened."

But later that night, after talking with his neighbor, Blake found out otherwise. Apparently the city had been swayed by dollar signs after all and was preparing to side with MacKenzie. Blake punched in A.J.'s number and waited impatiently for her to pick up. When she did, he dispensed with the formalities and got right to the heart of the issue.

"A.J.? Blake. Looks like what George overheard is correct. My neighbor tells me that the board is prepared to proceed with TIF and give MacKenzie the green light to develop."

"Oh, Blake! We can't let that happen!"

He heard the dismay in her voice. "I'm not sure we can do much more," he said, his own voice tinged with discouragement.

"Well, at least we can have another meeting to discuss options. I'll call everyone tonight and see if we can get together tomorrow after we close. Aunt Jo wouldn't want us to give up without doing everything we can. And I feel the same way."

So did Blake. But he was beginning to think it was a lost cause.

"But how can they do that? Everyone was on our side!"

Somehow Blake had found himself up front with A.J. at the meeting, and he turned to respond to Rose. "Unfortunately, it's not being put to a vote. The alderman for this ward supports our cause, but the others apparently don't."

"I think it's time to call my nephew at the TV station," Joe said emphatically.

A.J. recalled the advice Blake's parents had given them at dinner. "But they won't come unless there's an event of some kind to cover."

"Then we make an event!" George declared.

"I think we should organize a protest," Alene said.

A.J. glanced at Blake. His jaw had tightened, and he was frowning. Which didn't surprise her. This had to be like a flashback from his parents' hippie days. The days he had hated.

"That's a good idea," Steve chimed in. "I know we could get a lot of the area residents to join us."

"The sooner the better," Carlos added.

"So, is everyone agreed on this course of action?" A.J. asked. Everyone nodded except Blake. "Okay, it looks like we have a consensus. Let's try to set this up for next Saturday. Can we pull it off that fast?"

"I think we have to," Rose said.

"Then Saturday it is. Now let's work out the details and the assignments."

By the time the meeting broke up half an hour later, they had a solid plan of action in place. As everyone filed out and A.J. locked the door, she turned around to find Blake watching her, a troubled expression on his face. Slowly she walked toward him. "I'm sorry, Blake. I know this isn't your thing."

He raked his fingers through his hair and shook his head. "I'm not sure I can do this, A.J. I want to save Turning Leaves as much as you do, but this…it's just not me."

"I know."

He shoved his fists into his pockets and gave a frustrated sigh. "I want to support what the group is doing. But the idea of marching around with a sign and having a TV news camera shoved in my face…I just don't know."

A.J. moved behind the desk and perched on the stool. She rested her elbows on the counter and propped her chin in her hands. Her eyes were sympathetic when she spoke. "You have to do what's right for you, Blake."

He looked at her. "Do you want to do this?"

"Not particularly. But this will certainly get the board's attention. I don't see any other way to convince them."

"I don't, either."

"You shouldn't do this if you don't want to."

"Jo would have."

"I know. But she didn't have your issues."

Blake studied A.J. for a moment. "How will you feel if I don't go?"

She was surprised by the question. "Does that matter?"

Like it or not, Blake realized he cared what A.J. thought. And he didn't want to disappoint her. "Yeah, it does."

A.J. considered the question. "I'll understand," she said finally.

"The others won't."

She shrugged. "We're all products of our past, Blake. So we shouldn't be too quick to judge what others do, or their motivations. You've worked hard on this cause, and you already left your comfort zone once—when you took my place at the meeting. Maybe that's enough."

As A.J. stood and began to turn out the lights in the shop, Blake considered her comment. Maybe she was right. Maybe he had done enough.

But deep in his heart, he didn't think that was true. Because this was the real test of his convictions. If you believed in something strongly enough, you had to take a stand. No matter the cost.

Just like A.J. had done on her trip to Washington.

The turnout on Saturday was better than anyone predicted, aided by remarkably fine weather for late March. Several hundred people milled about in front of city hall, and dozens carried signs protesting the new development.

Including Blake.

He'd spent several restless nights debating whether to participate. But in the end, he couldn't sit this one out. He'd poured the last three years of his life into Turning Leaves. The other merchants had invested many more in their businesses. Jo had believed in this area, and had worked hard to preserve its unique character and integrity. Now A.J. had taken on her cause. He had to do his part.

And oddly enough, it wasn't so bad. A number of people recognized him from the board meeting and had stopped to compliment him and offer their support. Even the presence of the news media didn't bother him. He let the other merchants do the talking on camera, but he really didn't care if his face was on the five o'clock news. Because he felt part of something important. Something bigger than himself. Something that linked all of these diverse people in a joint purpose. And it was a heartwarming feeling, one he'd never before experienced. He still had no confidence that city hall would ultimately put civic integrity above hard cash. But at least they would be able to say they'd tried their best to do the right thing. And that felt good.

"How are you holding up?"

Blake turned at A.J.'s voice, and his lips tipped into a wry smile. "My parents would be proud."

Her answering smile warmed his heart. As did the expression in her eyes, which spoke of admiration and respect. And something more, something indefinable, that made his throat go dry. "I'm sure they would," she replied softly, her voice slightly uneven. "And so am I."

She was pulled away then by a reporter, but as Blake watched her go, he suddenly felt more alive than he had in a very long time.

* * *

The atmosphere was festive that night, almost boisterous, as the merchants gathered in the bar at George's restaurant to watch the evening news together. But silence fell when the announcer introduced their story.

The camera panned the area in front of city hall, taking in the impressive crowd. A voice-over gave the background on the development proposal, and then a number of residents and merchants spoke on camera. There was an interview with Stuart MacKenzie, followed by one with the mayor, who assured the reporter that the voices of the protesters had been heard and that the board members would take their concerns under advisement when a final decision was made.

As the anchorman moved on to the next story, George turned down the volume and looked at A.J. "So what do you think?"

"I think we did everything we could. It was a positive story for us."

"So what do we do now?" Rose asked.

For some reason, everyone looked at Blake. Maybe because he had the closest connection to city hall. He wished he could offer them more, but he could only repeat what he'd told A.J. when she'd asked that question much earlier in the process.

"We wait."

Waiting wasn't easy, however. Almost every day the merchants checked in with one another, and Blake kept in close touch with his neighbor. But one week, then two, then three passed, and still there was no decision.

In the meantime, A.J. began to realize that she and Blake were becoming a couple. She wasn't exactly sure how that had happened. She supposed it had started when he began to regularly attend church services with her, after the blizzard. That had become a Sunday ritual, followed by breakfast together. Then she had started inviting him to dinner on a regular basis. He began bringing in lunch for them at the shop. They attended several movies together that they both wanted to see. He claimed it helped them relax as they waited for the verdict from the board.

It was always Dutch treat, so it wasn't exactly dating. And there was no romance involved. But an attraction simmered just below the surface. She was aware of it. And she was sure he was, too. One day soon they'd have to deal with it. But neither seemed ready to take that step.

Though they were especially careful at the shop to keep things purely professional, Nancy was too sharp to miss the change in their relationship.

"Things seem a little…friendlier…between you and Blake lately," she ventured one day in mid-April when she and A.J. were shelving some new arrivals.

A.J. reached for another stack of books, using the maneuver to hide her suddenly flushed face. "Well, we're very different. I suppose we're finally figuring out how to work together," she replied, striving for a matter-of-fact tone.

"That's good. Where is he, by the way? He's been gone an awfully long time."

A.J. glanced at her watch and frowned. "I don't

know. He said he was just going to grab a sandwich at the deli. Maybe he decided to eat at one of the tables in front." She gazed wistfully out the window. "I certainly would have. It's such a gorgeous day. Too gorgeous to waste inside."

"My sentiments exactly."

The women turned toward the back room. Blake was standing in the doorway with a wicker picnic hamper in his hand.

"What's that for?" Nancy asked.

"What do you think it's for?" He was grinning.

"Where did you get it?"

"Rose came to my rescue again."

A.J. stared at him. "You're going on a picnic?"

"Yes."

"But…aren't you scheduled to work this afternoon?"

"Nancy's here. And I called Trish. She's off from school today and can be here in half an hour. As you just said, this is much too nice a day to waste inside. The dogwoods are blooming, and the spring flowers are out in full force. I thought I'd head over to Tilles Park. Sit by the lake. Feed the ducks. Enjoy the sun."

Now it was Nancy's turn to stare. "Since when have you started noticing the beauty of nature? And skipping out on work?"

He shrugged. "I thought I'd give this spontaneous thing a shot." He turned to A.J. and gave her an engaging grin. "Want to join me?"

She continued to stare. She'd never seen him like this. "But…but I'm not sure we should just leave the shop…"

"Loosen up, A.J. The world won't end if we take the

afternoon off. Nancy can handle things. Right, Nancy?"

The woman looked from Blake to A.J., then back again, clearly bewildered. "Sure."

"See? So what do you say?"

A.J. knew a stack of invoices in the back needed processing. She was also supposed to change the window display this afternoon. And she had a new shipment of merchandise from Good Samaritan to unpack. There was way too much to do today to take the afternoon off. She hesitated, torn between her responsibilities at the shop and the appeal of Blake's invitation.

"Come on, A.J. Seize the moment." Blake's eyes were twinkling, and he winked at her.

The irony of his remark wasn't lost on her. It sounded like one of the lines she'd used on him when she'd first arrived. A wry smile tugged at the corners of her mouth. "I may regret this when I have to work till midnight tomorrow, but…okay."

"Terrific!" He reached for her hand and pulled her toward the back, talking to Nancy over his shoulder as A.J. grabbed her sweater. "I'm getting her out of here before she changes her mind. You've got my cell phone number if there's an emergency, right?"

"Don't worry about a thing. Just have fun."

Once they were in the car, A.J. turned to Blake. "So what's this all about?"

"What do you mean?"

"You've never done anything like this before."

"Are you complaining?"

"No. But it just seems a little…out of character."

He shrugged. "Maybe I'm changing."

She thought about that for a moment. "Well, don't change too much."

"You mean you liked that uptight, stuffy, inflexible, conventional guy you first met?"

She flushed. "I never said you were like that."

"You didn't have to. That's what you thought. And you were right. I did need to loosen up. To be more open to change. More spontaneous. So how am I doing?"

She smiled. Actually, Blake had been slowly changing over the past few months. He was starting to let go of the tight control he'd always exercised over his life. To go with the flow a bit more. His involvement with the MacKenzie situation was a great example. He'd left his comfort zone, taken a chance, and found out it wasn't so bad after all. She was happy for him. The changes he was making would surely enhance his life.

"You're doing great. But don't lose all your good qualities along the way, too, okay?"

"Such as?"

"Well, let's see." She ticked them off on her fingers. "You're dependable. Kind. Hardworking. Practical. Thoughtful. Smart."

"You forgot good-looking," he teased.

"Let's not get carried away," she replied with a grin.

"Ouch! You sure know how to hurt a guy." He turned into the park, made the loop to the lake and pulled into a parking space. "I just discovered this park. Rose told me about it a few days ago, so I checked it out. I can't believe I've lived here for three years and never even knew this place existed. But then, there were a lot of things I never noticed."

A.J. stepped out of the car and looked at the lake. A pavilion stood off to one side, and there was a large deck that went right up to the water. Built-in benches and picnic tables were scattered around the planked surface. "Well, I'm glad you noticed this," she said, smiling appreciatively at the peaceful, quiet scene.

"Yeah, and it's all ours today," he said, nodding toward the deserted pavilion.

Once again he reached for her hand, as he had at the shop. A.J. didn't protest. She liked the way his strong fingers held hers firmly, protectively.

He led her to a picnic table on the deck, near the water's edge. "How does this look?"

"Perfect."

"Okay. Let's see what Rose has packed." He opened the hamper and handed A.J. a checkered cloth. "Hmm. I see she expects us to do this in style. A tablecloth, no less." As A.J. spread the cloth, he rummaged around in the hamper, then began handing her the food. "Chicken salad on croissants. Pasta salad. Fresh fruit. Cheese and crackers. Double fudge brownies. Bottled water. I'd say we have a feast here."

"Seems like it."

A.J. unwrapped her sandwich and took a bite. She closed her eyes as she chewed, savoring the warm spring sun on her back and this stolen afternoon. "This is great!"

"So you don't mind playing hooky after all?" Blake teased, spearing a forkful of pasta salad.

"That's the trouble. I could do this every day. You're going to instill bad habits in me."

"I don't think that's possible."

"You might be surprised. You could turn me into a world-class loafer with no problem."

"Sorry. Don't buy it. There's not a lazy bone in your body."

"Mmm. I don't know. I feel pretty lazy today."

"That's probably because you need a day off."

"I'm off every Sunday. And every other Saturday."

"I mean a real vacation day."

She shrugged. "There's been a lot to learn at the shop. And things have been hopping with MacKenzie. Besides, who are you to talk? You don't take much time off. And I saw your calendar in the den when I spent the night at your house. Even on your free Saturdays you're busy." She turned to look at him. "I didn't know about the homeless shelter or Big Brothers until then. I'm impressed, Blake."

He dismissed her comment with a wave of his hand. "My paltry efforts pale in comparison to what you did in Afghanistan."

A troubled frown creased her brow. "Actually, I'm not sure I can take a lot of credit for that. Lately I've been doing a lot of soul-searching. In some ways, I think I was running away."

"You could have run to a safer, more comfortable place," he said skeptically.

"Maybe. But I wanted to go somewhere that didn't even remotely remind me of home."

"You picked a good place, then. And frankly, you had a lot to run away from."

She picked at her pasta salad with the tines of her fork. "Yeah, but running isn't the answer. Not in the long term," she said quietly, a touch of melancholy in her tone. She speared a forkful of noodles, and when she spoke again, her voice was more normal. "I'm not sorry I went to Afghanistan, though. We did some great work there. But I realize now that you don't have to go to the remote corners of the world to help others. You can do good work a lot closer to home. Like you do, with those two organizations."

"I'm just glad that another trip to Afghanistan isn't in your plans. Do you want a brownie?"

She grinned. "Are you kidding?"

He handed one over, then unwrapped his own. "By the way, I wanted to thank you for dragging me along to church that Sunday after the snowstorm."

"I don't recall dragging you. In fact, I think it was your idea."

"Well, maybe. But not for the most noble reasons." He hurried on before she could ask what he meant. "Anyway, I wanted to let you know that I took your advice and had a theological discussion with Reverend Matthews. In fact, more than one discussion."

She looked at him in surprise. "When did you do that?"

"The week after the storm. He was very approachable. And very informative."

"He's a great guy."

"Anyway, after that I called my parents."

She gave him a radiant smile. "Oh, Blake, I'm so glad! I bet they were delighted!"

He crumpled the plastic wrap from his brownie self-consciously. "Yeah, they were. We had a long talk. They want me to come and visit."

"Are you going to go?"

"Probably. I didn't commit, but I think it makes sense. It's hard to really connect by phone. We made a good start, though."

She reached over impulsively and laid her hand on his. "I'm so happy for you, Blake. And proud of you. It's not easy to forgive, to let go of resentment that goes so deep. Especially when you've felt that way for such a long time. But at least you've taken the first step. Started the healing process. The rest will be easier."

Blake looked down at A.J.'s hand resting on his, her slender fingers pale against his darker skin. Then he glanced at her face. Her earnest eyes reflected absolute happiness for him and her lips were turned up softly into a tender smile that tugged at his heart. The sun lit up the red highlights in her hair, and Blake drew an unsteady breath. He hadn't asked A.J. on this picnic for romantic reasons. At least not consciously. He'd simply wanted to get away from worries about MacKenzie for a few hours, and to share the beautiful day with her—as well as the news of the first steps he'd taken with his faith and with his parents. But now he realized that without her, he wouldn't even have appreciated the beauty of this day. Or considered going to church. Or initiated contact with his parents. Or found himself on a picket line. Or planned an impromptu picnic.

After meeting A.J., Blake had quickly realized that she was going to make changes. In the shop, and in his life. He'd resisted those changes every step of the way. Had feared them. But now he realized that the changes she'd made breathed new life into his mind—and his heart. And he also realized something else.

He was a goner.

His gaze returned to her face. Her smile had faded, and there was uncertainty in her eyes as she sensed the shift in his mood. He also saw fear. Which he understood. Giving your heart to someone special, then losing that person, would breed fear. And he was afraid, too. Of trusting. Of putting his welfare in someone else's hands. Perhaps that was why he'd never married. Why he'd never even gotten serious about any of the women he'd dated.

Until now.

Blake stared at A.J., a woman he had once considered the most unlikely possible candidate for a wife. Just a few months ago he had wanted to wring her neck. When had his feelings grown so serious? All he knew was that thanks to Jo—and maybe to an even higher power—this special woman had come into his life. Yes, they were different. Yes, they had disagreements. Yes, they were bound to clash. But they were both changing. They were beginning to recognize and value the unique qualities they each brought to their relationship. And they absolutely could not deny the chemistry between them. They'd certainly tried to. But it was growing stronger every day. And they needed to deal with it.

Slowly Blake turned to straddle the bench, his gaze never leaving her face. He saw the sudden rush of fear in her eyes. But he also saw the yearning.

"Blake, I…"

His fingers on her lips instantly silenced her, and she went absolutely still. "I know. You're scared. So am I," he said huskily. "I never planned this, never in a million years expected it. But there's something between us, A.J. I know you feel it, too. I see it in your eyes."

"Th-that doesn't mean we should do anything about it."

He reached over and gently brushed a stray tendril of hair off her face. "Do we have a choice?"

She didn't respond immediately. When she did speak, her voice was choked. "I c-can't take the chance. It h-hurts too much to l-lose someone you love. I wouldn't survive…again."

With his free hand he reached for hers and comfortingly stroked the back with his thumb. "Does it hurt any less to be alone?" he asked gently.

When she didn't respond, he reached over and rested his hands on her stiff shoulders. He could feel her quivering, and he kneaded her taut muscles, realizing his own hands were none too steady.

"You know I would never hurt you, don't you?" he said softly.

"Not on purpose. Eric wouldn't have, either. That doesn't make it hurt any less when someone is gone. And life doesn't come with guarantees."

He had no response to that. Because it was true.

"Besides, w-we're too different," she said unevenly.

That was something he *could* respond to. "What's that old saying about opposites attracting?"

"I—I'm not sure I ever believed that."

"Me neither. Until now. Besides, I don't think we're as different as we once thought. And the differences we do have seem to complement each other. That's not a bad thing, is it?"

"I guess not."

"Besides, after one kiss the attraction might fizzle anyway. Then our problem is solved."

She managed the ghost of a smile. "This is sure an odd conversation."

His own lips quirked up wryly. "Well, our relationship hasn't exactly developed along conventional lines. Why start following the norm now?"

He felt the tension in her shoulders ease slightly.

"I'm not even sure I remember how to do this," she said with disarming honesty. "It's been a long time. You'll probably be disappointed."

He lifted one hand from her shoulder and traced the outline of her face with a gentle finger. "I doubt that." When he touched her lips, she drew in a sharp breath. "Come here. Let me hold you for a minute." Without waiting for her to respond, he closed the distance between them and pulled her close, cradling her head against his shoulder. It was an embrace of comfort and reassurance—but unlike the other times he'd held her, it was also an embrace of anticipation.

He stayed like that for what seemed to be a long time, stroking her back, communicating to her by his gentle but strong touch that she had nothing to fear from him. That he understood her apprehensions, and the need to take things slowly. For both their sakes. But that it was also time to begin exploring the attraction between them.

Blake wasn't sure if her trembling actually subsided, or if he only imagined it had. But finally he turned his head and let his lips make contact with her temple, then slowly travel across her forehead. When he felt her hands lightly, tentatively, touch his back, he moved slightly away and cradled her head with one hand, resting the other lightly on her shoulder. He was careful to communicate through his posture that she could move away at any time. If she kissed him back, he wanted it to be freely given.

He waited a moment, until her eyelids flickered open and he saw what he needed to see. Then, his gaze never leaving hers, he slowly closed the distance between them until their lips connected. He brushed his lips across hers, once, twice, three times, light as a summer breeze. Waiting for a reaction. Giving her a chance to pull back.

But she didn't. Instead, she pulled him closer. And Blake needed no more encouragement. Telling himself to move slowly, he tenderly claimed A.J.'s sweet lips.

After an interlude in which time seemed to stand still, Blake finally broke contact. He backed off slightly and gazed down at her, gripping her upper arms. She wasn't sure if he was trying to steady himself or her. No matter. They both needed to regain their balance.

"Wow!" A.J. whispered, her eyes wide.

"Yeah. Wow!"

She took a deep breath. "So what do we do now?"

When his eyes darkened in response and he leaned toward her, she put a restraining hand on his chest. "Not a good idea."

He sighed and backed off, flashing her a grin. "Yeah. You're right. But we can't ignore this, you know."

"I know. It's just that…" Her voice trailed off.

"You need to move slowly," he finished for her.

She nodded. "I still have issues to work through. In spite of what just happened, I'm still scared."

"I understand. I've never been a fast mover, either. Remember, I'm just starting to dabble in spontaneity. We both need time to sort things out. We'll take it slow and easy. Okay?" He reached for her hands.

She looked at him skeptically. "Do you think we'll be able to manage that?"

A smile tugged at the corners of his mouth. "We're both disciplined people. We can make this work."

"So…no more kissing?" she said wistfully.

He smiled. "I wouldn't go that far. Let's try this."

He leaned toward her, keeping her hands in his, and kissed her tenderly. It was a kiss that spoke of honor and caring and attraction.

"How's that?" he asked when he finally moved away.

She drew an unsteady breath. "This isn't going to be easy."

"I know. But we can do this, A.J. Trust me."

She gazed into his eyes and smiled. "I do."

But as they gathered up the remnants of their picnic, he hoped her confidence wasn't misplaced. Because he knew his self-discipline was about to be mightily tested. So Blake did something he'd never done in his life. He asked for help from a higher power.

Lord, I know I'm new to the fold. I don't even know how to pray yet. But I hope You'll listen to my request anyway. I'm not sure where this thing with A.J. is headed. But I know I'm falling in love with her. I don't honestly know whether that's in either of our best interests. So we need to give this time, and not get so caught up in the chemistry between us that we're blind to more important considerations. You know I've always been good at self-control. Probably too good. But I need it now. Big-time.

And Lord, I ask for Your guidance as we start down this new path. Help us both to know Your will and to make good decisions. A.J. doesn't need to be hurt again, and I don't need to make any more mistakes with people I care about. So please watch over us.

Blake had no idea if his plea was heard. But according to Reverend Matthews, God was receptive to any communication that came from the heart. And his certainly had. Because for the first time in years, he was willing to admit that he needed assistance.

Blake recalled the day A.J. was on the ladder, when he'd told her that it was okay to ask for help. He realized now that she could have thrown that comment right back at him. He was just as bad as she was in that regard, for different reasons. She refused help because she didn't want to rely on someone who might be taken away from her. Blake's self-reliance had been forged in his childhood, when he'd resolved to take control of his own destiny so that he would never again have to depend on anyone for food or housing.

But as he was slowly coming to realize, security and stability came in many forms. The material kind wasn't all that permanent and durable, no matter how well you planned. Look at his friend, Jack. He'd recently lost his job after twelve years because of a corporate reorganization. And he had two kids, a mortgage and a wife who was a stay-at-home mom. From a material perspective, his world had just caved in, his security and stability gone in the blink of an eye. But when Blake had spoken with him a few days before, Jack had been confident that things would work out. After all, as he'd told Blake, "I have my faith and my family. I'm still a rich man, buddy." Family and faith. The very things that A.J. said had seen her through the crises in her life. Maybe he'd been looking in the wrong places for security and stability all along.

He still believed self-reliance was a good thing. But maybe it was time to admit he needed other people in his life. His friends. His family. A.J.

And God.

Chapter Ten

"Thank you for seeing me, Reverend Matthews."

The minister extended his hand to A.J. "It's my pleasure. Sorry to keep you waiting. We have a very active five-year-old, and my wife needed a second pair of hands this morning. She's getting over a bad cold and isn't quite up to full speed yet."

"No problem. I hope she feels better soon."

He grinned and took a seat at right angles to hers. "There's no keeping Sam down for long." The love in his eyes when he spoke of Samantha touched A.J. She'd gotten to know the minister's red-haired wife over the past few months, and the obvious mutual affection between Reverend Matthews and his spouse always reminded her of her relationship with Eric.

"So, what can I do for you on this beautiful spring day?" the minister continued.

A.J. took a deep breath. "I could use some advice."

"I'll do my best."

Encouraged by his insightful questions, A.J. told him her story. Of her engagement, Eric's death, her injuries, her years in Afghanistan, her work with Good Samaritan. And more recently, of Aunt Jo's legacy and her partnership with Blake.

"That's quite a story, A.J.," the minister said when she finished. "It sounds like your life is on a new and satisfying track. Your faith seems strong. So what brings you to me today?"

She glanced down and played with her purse clasp, and when she spoke her voice was subdued. "I'm not so sure about the faith part."

"Tell me about it."

She looked over at Reverend Matthews, wondering if he would judge her lacking when she admitted that she hadn't put her life fully in the Lord's hands. And how could a minister, a man of deep faith who was so happily married, understand her fears about commitment—to people or to plans?

He spoke comfortingly, as if he'd read her mind. "No one's faith is perfect, A.J."

She took a shaky breath. "It's just that…well, ever since the accident I've lived kind of a vagabond lifestyle and avoided putting down any roots. I told myself that I was trying to remain unencumbered so that I could be open to God's call and totally available to do His will. But lately, I've been thinking that maybe I've been fooling myself. That maybe…maybe I'm just afraid. Putting down roots means that you're willing to make plans for the future and to trust that no matter what happens with those plans, God will be there to comfort you and guide you. But if you don't stay in any one place long enough to make commitments or plans, you don't have to put that belief to the test."

He leaned forward intently and clasped his hands between his knees. "I can see that you're deeply troubled by this."

"I am. I always thought my faith was strong. That I had absolute trust in the Lord. Now I'm not so sure."

"Perhaps you can take some comfort in knowing that you're not alone with this struggle. Think of the story of the apostles when they were out in the boat with the Lord during the storm on the lake. They doubted and were afraid. Or the time our Lord told Peter to walk to Him across the water. When Peter's trust faltered, when he began to doubt, he started to sink. That happens to all of us, A.J. It's not a sign of weak faith. It's a sign of being human. From the story you've just told me, I'd say your faith has sustained you well through some turbulent times. So I have a feeling that your doubts are of a more recent vintage." He paused a moment. "Would Blake have anything to do with this?" he asked gently.

She nodded slowly. "I think I might be…my feelings for him are…growing every day. But we're so different. That scares me. And I'm afraid to take another chance on love. I thought I would die when I lost Eric. I'm afraid I might not survive that kind of trauma again." She gazed at him, thought of his perfect family, and sighed. "I guess that might be hard for you to understand."

A fleeting echo of pain swept across his eyes. "Actually, it's not," he said quietly. "I lost my first wife not long after we were married. An aneurysm. It took her instantly, with no warning. So I've known dark days, too—days when I doubted and was afraid. I never expected to marry again. I never even wanted to. Then Sam came into my life. We were very different people, and we both had unresolved issues. We fought the attraction, but in the end we recognized that our love was a gift. It didn't come with guarantees, but most things in life don't."

A.J. stared at the man across from her. She'd always thought he looked too young to have those streaks of silver at his temples. Now she knew what had put them there. "I'm so sorry," she whispered.

"Thank you. Loss is a very difficult thing to deal with. And it can destroy us, if we let it. But it doesn't have to. My life is happy now. Because Sam and I realized that it was better to put our trust in God and accept the gift of our love for as long as He blessed us with it than to spend the rest of our lives alone."

A.J. frowned. "Blake said almost the same thing."

"He's a wise man."

"He told me he's spent some time with you."

Reverend Matthews chuckled. "He certainly keeps me on my toes. He asks probing questions that have on more than one occasion sent me to my library to do research. But I'd rather have one believer like him, who deals directly with questions and is eager to learn about the faith, than a dozen who accept blindly. If he chooses to become a Christian, his faith will be strong. Because he will have made an informed decision. He's a good man, A.J."

"I know." She took a deep breath. "Thank you, Reverend Matthews."

"I'm always here if you need me. Shall we take a moment to talk with the Lord before you leave?"

She nodded, and he reached for her hand as they bowed their heads.

"Lord, let us feel Your presence, so that doubts may disappear. Give us the wisdom to discern Your will and the courage to follow it. Guide our steps on this difficult journey of life, and steady us when we stumble. Let us feel Your infinite love and compassion, and let us take comfort in the knowledge that You understand and forgive our mistakes. Help us to savor each day as a precious gift, and not let anxieties about the future overwhelm us. Bless A.J. with Your grace as she struggles to hear Your voice. Help her put her trust in You so that she may feel the peace that comes with surrender. And help her let go of her fear of the future so that she may live fully today. We ask this through Christ our Lord."

For a long moment, A.J. left her eyes closed. Reverend Matthews's prayer had been simple. But it had come from the heart. And it had touched on all of her fears. When she finally gazed at the man across from her, she saw no reproach in his eyes because of the doubts she'd expressed. She saw only a deep compassion and empathy that communicated more eloquently than words how well he understood exactly what was in her heart.

And if he could understand, surely so could God.

That thought came to her suddenly, like a shaft of sunlight that streams through dark storm clouds and illuminates the world. A gentle, freeing peace stole over her as the guilt raised by her doubts dissipated, leaving her soul quiet and serene. And in that stillness, she knew God would speak to her. She had only to listen for His voice.

The doorbell rang, and A.J. smiled as she wiped her hands on a kitchen towel, then glanced at the clock. Nine o'clock on the dot. Blake may have gotten more spontaneous in the past few months, but he was still Mr. Punctuality. Which she appreciated even more since he'd told her that he thought tardiness indicated a lack of respect for the other person's time. She admired his consideration. And so many other things.

The moment she opened the door he pulled her into his arms and greeted her with a tender kiss.

When he released her, she smiled at him, her arms still looped around his neck. "You'll give poor Mr. Simmons a heart attack," she murmured, catching a glimpse of her neighbor peering through a crack in his door.

"Can't be helped," he said. "I figured it was safer to kiss you out here."

She chuckled and reached for his hand. "Come on in. I'm almost ready."

Blake followed her, and almost fell over a small, shaggy dog sitting patiently inside the door. "What's this?" he asked in surprise.

She grinned. "Blake, meet Felix. I rescued him from the pound yesterday."

"Isn't Felix a cat's name?"

She planted her hands on her hips and gave him a

teasing grin. "Are you still hung up on that name thing?"

He smiled. "Touché." He squatted down and reached over to scratch the dog's head. "Hey, Felix." He looked the dog over. "What is he?"

"A mutt. He's about five years old. Apparently he'd been on the streets, just wandering around for a while. They told me at the pound that not many people want older dogs. But I thought he was perfect. Besides, he looked like he needed a friend."

"And the apartment was okay with this?"

"Yeah. For a hefty deposit. But he's worth it. I fell in love with him the minute I saw him."

Blake stood and turned to A.J. "So what prompted this?"

She shrugged. "Companionship."

"Are you feeling lonesome?" His tone was teasing, but there was something serious in his eyes. A.J. knew he was purposely letting her set the pace in their relationship. At the same time, she knew that a day of reckoning was coming.

"Not anymore. Felix took care of the problem. He's the perfect companion. And he never talks back."

"Are you telling me you like the shaggy, silent type? I could let my hair grow."

A.J. giggled. "Very funny. Let me grab a hat and I'll be right with you," she said over her shoulder as she headed down the hall.

Blake gave Felix another scratch, then wandered over to the dinette table, which was littered with notes and documents. He saw the name of their church on several sheets, and realized that the papers had something to do with the long-range plan Brad Matthews had mentioned from the pulpit a few times. The minister had said there was a committee working on a variety of projects, including a capital campaign.

"Okay, I'm all set."

Blake turned. Between the kiss and the dog, he hadn't really paid any attention to what A.J. was wearing. Now his gaze took in her calf-length dress in shades of purple, which he'd swear was tie-dyed. A macramé purse was slung over her shoulder, and she held a large straw hat. At one time, he would have thought her outfit was weird. But now he realized it wasn't weird at all. It was just A.J. And it suited her. Perfectly.

"You look very nice."

"Thanks. I found a great new vintage clothing store."

"What's all this?" He nodded to the paperwork on the table.

"Reverend Matthews asked me if I'd serve on the long-range planning committee for the church. It's a three-year term, so I wasn't sure at first. But I finally agreed." She glanced at her watch. "We'd better go or we'll be late for the service."

Blake followed her to the door, processing the latest developments. A.J. had bought a dog. Which meant she'd made a commitment to let another living thing into her life. And she'd agreed to serve on the committee. Which meant she was planning to be around for at least three years.

Blake had been asking for guidance about how quickly to proceed with A.J., praying for a sign that she was ready for what he wanted to do next. Today he'd been given two signs. It was time for the next step.

"Sorry I'm late. I got hung up."

A.J. glanced up from the computer where she was entering orders. "No problem. Did you get your business taken care of?"

Blake stuck his hand in his pocket and fingered the small box from the jeweler. He'd dropped his grandmother's engagement ring off the week before to have it cleaned and polished, and they'd done a superb job restoring the vintage piece. Blake had no idea if A.J. would like the old-fashioned setting, but he was perfectly willing to have the stones refitted if that's what she preferred. His only concern was whether she was ready to accept the ring at all.

"Blake?"

A.J. was eyeing him strangely.

"Yeah. Yeah, I got everything taken care of. Listen, what are you doing tonight?"

"Making some desserts for the church picnic tomorrow."

"Could I tempt you with dinner out instead? We could pick up something at the bakery for the church."

There was an odd electricity in the air. A peculiar tension. A.J. looked at Blake curiously. "Is something wrong?"

"No. I just thought it might be nice to have dinner together. We don't get to do that very often on weekdays."

That was true. She or Blake, or both, were usually

at the shop till closing. *The shop*. Maybe that was it, she speculated. The end of their six-month partnership was looming, a fact that had hit home when she'd turned her calendar over to May yesterday. Just four weeks remained. Neither she nor Blake had talked about what would happen at the end of the month—assuming, of course, that the MacKenzie deal fell through and they still *had* a shop. But it was on her mind. A lot. She'd agreed at the beginning to consider selling Blake her half ownership. However, she had grown to love the business.

As well as the man who'd come with it.

And she had a feeling Blake felt the same way.

Maybe that's what this dinner was about, she speculated, as her heart tripped into double time. Even though no words of love had been uttered, she'd begun to let herself think about a life with Blake, to make some preliminary plans. Very preliminary. Frankly, she wasn't sure she was ready for a discussion about either their relationship or the shop, but they'd have to talk both things over sooner or later. It might as well be tonight.

"Okay. What time?"

"How does six-thirty sound?"

"I'll be ready."

And she was. Except Blake didn't show up at the appointed time. Or five minutes later. Or ten. Or fifteen. At which point A.J. began to panic. Blake was never late. And on the rare occasion when he was delayed for some reason, even for a few minutes, he called her. Always.

The phone rang just as A.J. was reaching for it to dial his number.

"Blake?"

He heard the breathlessness in her voice, knew that she'd been worried. "I'm okay, A.J. But my dad isn't. When I called out there a few minutes ago to confirm some things about my visit next week, I found out my dad had a heart attack today."

"Oh, Blake! How bad is it?"

"Apparently pretty mild. They weren't even going to call me about it. They said they didn't want me to worry, or to cancel my trip next week because he was sick. Listen, I need to go out there. Right away. I don't know if they're telling me the whole story, and if anything happened to my dad before…" His voice grew hoarse, and he stopped to clear his throat. "I just need to go."

"Of course."

"You'll be shorthanded at the shop."

"We'll cope."

"And the whole MacKenzie deal is still up in the air."

"You said yourself there's nothing we can do now but wait. And I'll let you know if I hear any news. Just go. Don't worry about anything here."

He sighed. "I'm sorry about this, A.J."

"Don't be. This is what you do for family. You go when they need you. You support them. You show them you care. I'd be disappointed if you didn't go."

"Thanks. We'll reschedule this when I get back. Okay?"

"Absolutely. Did you call the airline yet?"

"No. That's next on my list."

"Let me know when your flight is. I'll drive you."

"You don't have to do that."

"I want to. No arguments."

He didn't even try to dissuade her. She obviously wasn't going to budge. Besides, he wanted to see her before he left.

He was on the cell phone most of the way to the airport, arranging for a rental car in Oregon, calling in regrets for a board meeting with Big Brothers, canceling an appointment he had with Reverend Matthews. She stole a few worried glances at him during the drive. He looked more harried than she'd ever seen him, and the deep creases in his brow told her just how upset he was about his father.

For safety's sake, he insisted she leave him at the drop-off area instead of parking in the garage, and she didn't argue. She stood quietly beside him as he took out his carry-on and glanced at his watch.

"You'd better go. This is cutting it pretty close already," she said.

Blake reached over and gently stroked her cheek. "This wasn't in my plans for tonight."

"You've gotten better about changing plans on short notice."

"I didn't want to change these." He studied her for a moment, as if memorizing her features, then reached over and pulled her close. For a long moment he just held her, drawing strength from her warm embrace. "I'll be back soon," he said, his voice muffled in her hair.

He backed up then, and she searched his face. The harsh overhead lights mercilessly highlighted the strain and tension in his features. Now it was her turn to touch his face.

"Take whatever time you need. I'll still be here when you get back."

"Is that a promise?"

There was more in his question than a mere confirmation that she would be physically there. And she knew it. But it didn't alter her response. "Yes."

His eyes darkened and he leaned toward her, his lips touching hers in a brief kiss.

"I—I'll be thinking about you," she whispered when he broke contact.

He took her hands in his, and his gaze locked with hers. "That's good. Because a man always likes to know that he's on the mind of the woman he loves."

Then, before she could respond, he reached for his bag and strode away.

"We appreciate your coming out, son. But you could have waited until next week, like you planned. We're sorry to inconvenience you."

Blake looked at his father and tried to swallow past the lump in his throat. He had gone directly to the hospital from the airport, mentally preparing himself for this scene along the way. But walking in and finding his robust father flat on his back and looking very frail and vulnerable had still shocked him. "It's not an inconvenience, Dad."

"Carl didn't even want me to call. But I thought you'd want to know. We didn't expect you to drop everything and come out, though."

He looked at his mother, who was sitting on the other side of his father's hospital bed, holding her husband's hand.

"I wanted to be here."

A look passed between Jan and Carl, and his mother's eyes filled with tears. His father patted her hand, then turned to Blake. His own eyes were suspiciously moist.

"I'll be fine, son. It will just take a little time."

Blake had spoken with the doctors, and while his father's prognosis was good, the heart attack had been more serious than his mother had led him to believe on the phone. Recovery would take more than a little time. Meaning that for the immediate future, his mother would be on her own to run the shops. Which he was confident she was perfectly capable of doing—under normal circumstances. But he wasn't so sure about right now, when she was worried about her husband.

"Can you stay for a few days, Li…Blake?"

He nodded slowly. "I'd like to spend some time with you. And visit your shops. Maybe I can even help out a little, since you'll be shorthanded."

Carl frowned. "This was supposed to be a vacation for you."

"We don't want to put you to work the minute you get here," his mother concurred.

He shrugged. "That's what family's for."

His mother hesitated and glanced uncertainly at Carl. "Well, second quarter closing will need to be taken care of in the next couple of weeks. Carl's always been our liaison with the accountants, but with your business background it might be helpful if you could look over their shoulder this one time."

"I can do that, Jan," Carl protested.

"I'll do it, Dad. You need to concentrate on getting better."

Jan swiped at her eyes, then impulsively reached across the bed with her free hand. Blake hesitated only a fraction of a second before he took it. And only a second more before he laid his other hand over his father's.

"I know we haven't been close," he said, his voice strangely tight. "And I know a lot of that—maybe all of it—is my fault. You've reached out to me many times through the years. I just haven't responded. And I'm sorry for that now."

"It was our fault, too, Blake. Your dad and I didn't do the best job raising you. We never realized how important stability is to a child. We thought that our lifestyle would expose you to new experiences and instill a sense of adventure in you. It was only years later, when I went back to school for nutrition and took some child psychology courses, that I realized how badly we'd failed. We never gave you the security you needed. But it was too late. You were already grown up."

His mother's voice broke, and Blake squeezed her hand.

"Mom, it's okay," he said, his own voice uneven. "I know you and Dad did your best."

"It wasn't good enough," his father said.

Blake looked over at his father. The older man's face was strained and pale, and he clearly wasn't up to all emotional scene tonight. But Blake wanted his parents to at least know that he was willing to do his part to mend the rift.

"It *was* good enough, Dad, because at the time, you and Mom thought you were doing the right thing. And it's not too late," he said, echoing words A.J. had once spoken to him. "I'm willing to start over, if you are."

Carl and Jan exchanged another look.

"It's what we've prayed for," she told Blake, dabbing at her eyes. "A second chance."

"We'll do better this time, son," his father said. "Everything will be different."

"Not everything," Jan corrected.

Blake looked at her curiously. "What do you mean?"

"We've always loved you, Blake. Maybe we haven't always shown it in the right way, or given you the things you needed, but you always had our love. You still do. That will never change."

Blake gazed from his mother to his father. The unconditional love and acceptance in their eyes made his throat tighten with emotion. Perhaps it had always been there and he'd just never noticed. Perhaps, through all these years when he'd felt so alone and adrift, he'd had a family after all, just waiting to be rediscovered.

Blake knew that the rebuilding process wouldn't happen overnight. He needed to learn how to relate to the two people across from him, who had clearly changed and grown through the years—just as he had. He needed to learn how to share his life with them. And he needed to learn how to say "I love you."

But tonight, as they sat with hands clasped in a sterile hospital room that served as a vivid reminder that no material security in the world could guarantee tomorrow, he knew they were on the road to creating the kind of security that money couldn't buy. A security that would transcend the constraints of time and space.

The security of a loving family.

And in his heart, Blake said a silent thank-you to the Lord for giving him the courage to take this first step toward forgiveness—and reconciliation.

He knew the road ahead wouldn't be easy. That they'd all make mistakes. After all, they were very different people. But so were he and A.J., and he'd fallen in love with her. So he knew he could make things work with his parents. That with love and commitment, they could create the kind of family that would sustain them in the years ahead.

And he also knew something else. Given how A.J. and his parents had hit it off, he'd never have to worry about his wife getting along with the in-laws!

If she said yes when he popped the question.

Which he intended to do as soon as possible.

Chapter Eleven

"**A.J.**! A.J.! Have you seen today's paper?"

A.J. looked up from the sales report she was studying. George stood in the office doorway, grinning broadly.

"No. Why?"

"We won! It is over. Here. Read." He thrust the newspaper at her and pointed to a small article in the metro section, which A.J. quickly scanned.

"The Maplewood Board of Aldermen has rejected a proposal by MacKenzie Properties, a prominent real estate development firm, to use Tax Increment Financing (TIF) as a basis for the construction of a new retail/residential complex in the 1200 block of Collier Avenue.

"'The development was strongly opposed by area merchants and residents, who circulated petitions and collected thousands of signatures. They also staged a rally in front of city hall a few weeks ago, which generated significant media attention. Mayor Lawrence Russell said that this strong opposition was the key factor in the board's decision.

"'The development would certainly have been good for Maplewood from a financial perspective, but one of the reasons our town has enjoyed such a phenomenal rebirth is because we have always maintained our neighborhood feel and preserved the integrity and character of the area,' Russell said. 'We hope to work with Mr. MacKenzie on other projects in the future, but we did not feel that this particular one was in the best interest of Maplewood, nor was it endorsed by our constituency.'

"Following the ruling, MacKenzie Properties withdrew its proposal for the development."

As she read, a smile spread over A.J.'s face. So David had triumphed over Goliath after all! She couldn't wait to tell Blake!

"I think we should celebrate," George said excitedly. "Tonight, we have a party at my restaurant. Come when you close. I tell the others." He looked around. "Where is Blake?"

"His father became ill suddenly and he had to go to the West Coast. But I'll call him right away."

"I am sorry to hear that. But you will come tonight, yes?"

She grinned. "I wouldn't miss it for the world!"

Blake leaned back in his chair, giving his eyes a momentary rest from the computer screen. He'd been studying the books for his parents' stores for the past

several hours in preparation for the second-quarter closing, and he was impressed.

Big-time.

They didn't just run a couple of stores. They ran a
thriving enterprise that had been approached by a major
corporation interested in buying them out and franchis-
ing.

Blake frowned. He was happy for his parents.
They'd mentioned at A.J.'s the night she'd invited them
to dinner that they'd been far more successful than
they'd ever dreamed. But he'd had no idea they were
this successful.

So successful, in fact, that it took both his mother and
father working more than full-time just to keep up with
the daily demands of the business. And his father was
in no condition to resume that kind of work schedule.
Nor would he be in the immediate future—if ever. He
was home from the hospital and had started cardiac
rehab, but the doctors had made it clear that he needed
to permanently adopt a slower-paced lifestyle. And in
light of the demands of their business, he knew that di-
rective was weighing heavily on the minds of his parents.

And on his.

It was obvious to Blake that his parents needed more
help than he could offer in a week or two. Not only because of the current crisis, but because the business
was rapidly becoming more complex and growing beyond the scope of their expertise. They needed a full-
time business manager. And they could certainly hire
one. But Blake had the credentials, and no one would

care more about the business than family. Or watch out for their interests with the same diligence. And that was important. Because as he'd looked through the books, it was obvious that while much had changed over the years, his parents still retained the sunny optimism of their youth and were always willing to give people the benefit of the doubt. Which was not a bad thing—in theory. But it had cost them on a number of occasions when fly-by-night suppliers had disappeared with their money. Blake wouldn't be such a soft touch. And unlike a hired business manager, he wouldn't just take orders; he'd watch out for the best interests of his parents, even if that meant going head-to-head with them about financially unstable suppliers or unsound business arrangements.

Blake tried to ignore the sense of duty tugging on his conscience. After all, this wasn't his business. It wasn't his problem. But a little voice told him otherwise, reminded him that if he was trying to rebuild a family, he needed to be there for his parents. Even if what that required wasn't in his plans.

And moving to Oregon to run a natural food business definitely wasn't in his plans.

Blake reached back and massaged his neck with one hand. From a practical standpoint, his parents' business was certainly more profitable than the bookshop and would provide him with more financial stability and security. But that no longer held the appeal it once had. It wasn't even a factor in his decision.

Because of A.J.

The mere thought of her brought a smile to his lips.

As they'd worked side by side over the past few months, he'd learned so much from her. About priorities, about letting go, and about what really counted. And along the way, he'd fallen in love with her. Deeply. Irrevocably. Forever. He loved her enthusiasm. Her energy. The way her eyes flashed with passion when she discussed her beliefs. Her eclectic taste in clothes. Her intelligence. Her courage. Her determination. Her deep faith. And the willingness she was beginning to exhibit to once again put down roots, make plans for the future and open herself to love.

And now this. If he decided to stay and help his parents, he'd have to ask her to change direction again, to leave the shop she had come to love. Just when its future had been secured.

It was ironic, really. In the beginning, he'd backed away from the MacKenzie fight. But gradually he'd been pulled into it, and by the end he'd been fighting as hard as anyone else to stop the development. Not only to protect Jo's legacy and his own future, but because it seemed the right thing to do. He'd always figured their odds of winning were marginal, at best. That they could very well lose the shop, be forced to start over. He hadn't wanted that to happen. Now, selfishly, he almost wished it had. Because it would make his decision about his parents' situation much easier.

Blake knew that A.J. had been surprised by his somewhat subdued mood when she'd called to tell him the news. He'd tried to be enthusiastic, but his own dilemma was weighing heavily on his mind. He'd attributed his less-than-thrilled response to tiredness and concern over his father, and A.J. had seemed to buy that explanation. But it was more than that.

Because if he stayed to help his parents, he'd have to ask A.J. to leave St. Louis and start over once more. It would be a huge sacrifice on her part. And it would have to be motivated by a deep, abiding love.

Blake knew A.J. loved him. But he also knew she was still scared. Even under the best of circumstances, making a commitment to him would require her to take a huge leap of faith.

And these weren't even close to the best of circumstances.

Lord, why does life have to be so complicated? he lamented silently. His conscience called him to do one thing; his heart, another. If he went with the call of his conscience, he knew that it would put A.J.'s love for him to the test.

And he was scared to death he would fail.

"You're offering to stay on as our business manager?"

His parents' faces reflected shock, and Blake shifted uncomfortably in the wooden chair at their kitchen table. "Yes. The doctors say you'll be fine, Dad, but it will take time. You'll need some help in the meantime. And frankly, long-term as well. Because your business is getting incredibly complex. You two have done an impressive job, but I've reviewed the operation, looked at all the financials, and you're at a point where you need a full-time business manager. You could hire a stranger, of course. Or I could step into the role. I'd be happy to give you a copy of my résumé if you want to review my qualifications." He flashed them a grin, hoping to lighten the atmosphere. But they continued to stare at him, dumbfounded.

Finally Carl glanced at Jan, then turned back to Blake. "I don't even know what to say."

"Blake, are you sure? What did A.J. say about this?"

Leave it to his mom to hone right in on the heart of his problem, he thought wryly. Over the past two weeks, as he'd reconnected with his parents, she'd quickly picked up on Blake's interest in their dinner hostess. And been delighted for him, even though he'd never said exactly how serious he was about A.J.

It had taken Blake much prayer and soul-searching—and a phone call to Reverend Matthews—before he had decided to make this offer. He'd also considered talking with A.J., asking her advice, but he knew she'd tell him to go with his conscience—because she would never put selfish desires above family obligations. If there was a need, you met it. Period. So he'd made the decision on his own. He knew she would understand; he just prayed that she would find the courage to trust in their love despite the change in plans.

"Yes, I'm sure. And I haven't spoken with A.J. about this."

Jan frowned, but didn't press him on the point. She looked at Carl and reached for his hand. "It's too much to ask." The comment was directed at her husband, not her son.

"I agree." Carl turned to Blake. "You're right about us needing help, son. With the way the business has grown, we've known for the past few months that we were starting to get in over our heads. But there's no way we'd ask you to step in. We can manage."

"You didn't ask. I offered."

"And we love you for it. But it's not the right thing for you. You love the bookshop. You've fought hard to save it. And you've built a wonderful life in St. Louis," Jan said. "This business was our dream, not yours. You need to follow your own path."

Blake studied the two people seated across from him. He wanted to accept their answer. It would be the easy way out. But he knew their decision was based on consideration for him, not their own needs. So he couldn't just walk away. Because with a little convincing, he was sure he could change their minds.

"I'll tell you what. I need to make a quick trip back to St. Louis this weekend and take care of a few things. Why don't you think it over and we can talk when I get back?"

"I doubt we'll change our minds," Carl said.

"All I ask is that you think about it."

"We will. Just don't worry about us while you're gone. We'll be fine," Jan said. "And be sure to tell A.J. hello for us. She's a very special young woman. "

Blake already knew that. What he didn't know was her answer to the question he planned to ask her as soon as he returned.

"Have you heard from Blake lately?"

A.J. set down the stack of books she was carrying and glanced at Nancy. "A couple of days ago. Between helping his mom take care of his dad, plus trying to get a handle on their business, he's been buried."

"What's the latest on his dad?"

"He's doing better, but he won't be back to full speed anytime soon."

"Did Blake say when he was coming back?"

"No."

A.J. turned away to help a customer, but her mind was on Blake. Though he called regularly, her conversations with him were generally brief and fairly impersonal. And he always sounded distracted and harried. Even the good news about the shop hadn't seemed to perk him up much. And while he never failed to say that he missed her, there had been no more mention of the "L" word.

A man always likes to know that he's on the mind of the woman he loves.

Blake's parting words to her at the airport echoed again in her mind, as they had constantly for the past two weeks. In between customers at the shop, at the church picnic, lying in bed late at night, they kept replaying. He hadn't had to worry. She'd thought of little but him. And the future.

A.J. was fairly certain that she and Blake were headed down a serious path. Serious enough to end in marriage. She also suspected that things would have moved more quickly in that direction if fear hadn't held her back. She was immensely grateful for Blake's patience as she dealt with her issues, and for his understanding that those issues had nothing to do with her feelings for him. They were born of trauma and tragedy and pain, and the overwhelming fear of loss. But she'd never forgotten the words Blake had once said to her when she'd talked of those fears. He'd simply asked, "Does it hurt any less to be alone?"

Slowly, as Blake had filled her life with warmth and laughter and caring, she'd found the answer to that question. The fear hadn't gone away completely; she didn't know if it ever would. But she did know that Blake had become an important part of her life. In fact, she could no longer imagine her life without him.

So she'd begun to think of the future they might share. And to make some tentative plans. And to eagerly wait for him to return.

The bell at the entrance jangled. A.J. looked up...and stopped breathing. Blake stood in the doorway, overnight case in hand, looking weary, worn—and utterly wonderful. She smiled at him, and his intimate answering smile warmed her all the way to her toes. And did funny things to her voice when she could finally find it. "Hi."

"Hi yourself."

"Welcome back, Blake," Nancy said.

With an obvious effort he dragged his gaze away from A.J. and looked at Nancy. "Thanks. How's everything been here?"

"We missed you."

"Did you?" He looked back at A.J., and his eyes darkened. Suddenly her heart lurched into a staccato beat.

Nancy nodded. "Yeah. We've been taking on extra hours, but I'll be glad to get back to a more normal schedule. Eileen will be glad, too. She misses her mom."

Blake took a closer look at A.J. There were fine lines at the corners of her eyes, and dark circles underneath. Obviously his absence had put a strain on everyone.

"Well, if you don't need me anymore, I'm going to take off, A.J. I can lock up as I leave."

It took a moment for Nancy's words to register, then A.J. frowned and glanced at her watch. "Oh. Right. It's time to close. That's fine, Nancy. You go ahead."

"Okay. See you later. Glad you're back, Blake."

"Thanks."

They heard her set the lock on the front door, and a moment later it clicked shut.

Slowly Blake put his suitcase down and walked toward A.J. His gaze never left hers as he took her hand and pulled her into the back room, then looped his arms around her waist. His eyes were only inches from hers. "Can I get a proper welcome now?" he said.

Without waiting for her to respond, his lips touched hers. A.J. surrendered to the kiss, wrapping her arms around his broad back. There was reunion and promise in the kiss they exchanged.

When it ended, Blake pulled her close. "It feels so good to be home."

She closed her eyes. Home was a good way to describe how she felt in Blake's arms. "I missed you. A lot."

A chuckle rumbled deep in his chest. "I sort of got that impression. But I'm glad you confirmed it. Could you tell I missed you?"

Now it was her turn to smile. "Just a little."

"Of course, you do have Felix to keep you company."

"Felix is great. But he falls short in several areas."

"Such as?"

"Well, he's not a great conversationalist. And he snores."

"So snoring is a bad thing?"

She backed up and gave him a look of mock horror. "Don't tell me you snore!"

"I don't think so. But my dad's snored for years. And Mom still loves him."

Suddenly serious, A.J. studied his face. He looked exhausted. "How is he doing?"

"Better. But he still has a long way to go."

"Did you have dinner?"

"I grabbed something at the airport."

"Why didn't you call? I would have picked you up."

"I figured you'd be here. And you're already short-handed."

"Would you like to come over to my place for a little while?"

He'd like nothing better. But he didn't want to be distracted from his plan for tonight. Regretfully he shook his head.

"I'm really beat. But I could use a cup of coffee. Is there any left in the pot out front?"

"I don't know. I haven't cleaned up out there yet."

"I'll take a look."

She restrained him with one hand. "Sit. I'll check. You look like you're ready to drop."

Blake didn't argue. Besides, he needed a moment to still the sudden pounding of his heart. He reached inside the pocket of his slacks and fingered the satin case, just to assure himself that the ring was still there. Then he took a deep breath and let it out slowly. He'd been waiting for this moment for weeks. Now that it was upon him, he was scared.

"Here you go."

A.J. deposited his coffee on the small lunch table in the back and sat beside him. He took a steadying sip, noting that his hand was trembling slightly. Which he supposed wasn't unusual when you were about to ask a woman to marry you.

"Are you going back?"

Carefully Blake set the cup on the table and looked at her. "Yes. I'm only here for the weekend. I'm really sorry to leave you shorthanded, A.J."

"Don't be. We can cope. How long will you need to stay?"

She didn't look put out. She didn't complain about the extra work at the shop. She didn't make an issue out of his extended absence. To her, it was a given. Family came first. He knew she believed that. But the strength of that belief was about to be tested.

Blake took a deep breath and reached for her hand, his gaze fixed on hers. "Possibly for a very long time." And then he filled her in.

As A.J. listened, the plans she'd let herself begin to think about slowly disintegrated and her world began to crumble. She'd been here before. And she hated it. Hated the feeling of helplessness. Of panic. Of sudden, overwhelming despair. She'd vowed once never to put herself in this position again. But she'd broken her own rule. She'd let Blake become such an integral part of her life that a future without him seemed empty and bleak. So the situation she now found herself in was her own fault. She had no one to blame but herself. She'd opened her heart to this man, and now he was going to break it and walk away.

As she looked at Blake's face, she knew that his decision had not come easily. She saw the conflict in the depths of his eyes, saw the lines of fatigue and strain at their corners, saw the deeply etched furrows in his brow. She tried to focus on his words, but as he concluded she knew she'd missed a lot.

"So I had to offer, A.J. They need me."

But so do I! she wanted to cry. Yet her spoken words were different. "I understand," she said numbly.

He stroked the back of her hand with his thumb, then made a move to stand. A.J. automatically began to follow suit, but he pressed her gently back and went down on one knee beside her. He cocooned both of her hands in his and gave her a shaky grin.

"Mr. Conventional to the end," he said, his voice slightly uneven. "I had planned to do this the night I left, in a more romantic spot with candlelight and flowers. But life has a funny way of changing plans. Besides, this is probably a more appropriate place, since the shop is what brought us together."

He paused and took a deep breath. "A.J., the life I'm about to offer you isn't the one I—or you—might have envisioned a couple of weeks ago. But it will still be good. Because we'll be together. And that's what really counts in the end. You told me once that home isn't so much a place—that it's simply being with the people you love. I believe that now. And I hope you still do, too.

"But I also know that you love Turning Leaves. I know that you're starting to build a life for yourself here. And I know that leaving all this behind, starting over yet again, will be a great sacrifice. So I want you to think about this very carefully. I don't want an answer tonight. Or even tomorrow, necessarily. Take whatever time you need."

He touched her cheek gently, then reached into his pocket and withdrew a small slip of paper.

"I spent a lot of time at the hospital while I was in Oregon, and sometimes, while my dad slept, I'd page through the Bible. I came across this passage from Jeremiah one day, and it really struck a chord with me. I wanted to share it with you." He glanced down and read in a slightly unsteady voice. "'For I know well the plans I have in mind for you, says the Lord, plans to give you a future full of hope.'" He paused, then looked back at her. "A.J., I have to tell you that you weren't in my plans. For years I'd been searching for a stereotype who fit all the conventional notions of what a wife should be. And then you came into my life and turned it upside down.

"For a long time I resented you. I liked my life just fine the way it was, and you were always changing things. But you know what? All of the changes you made were for the better. You opened my eyes to things

I'd never noticed before, challenged me to rethink long-held opinions, helped me discover the joy in spontaneity. You reminded me that I should never judge a book by its cover. And in keeping with the name of Jo's shop, you helped me turn over a new leaf.

"Slowly, kicking and dragging most of the way, I came to realize that maybe my plans weren't God's plans. And that His were better. Maybe that's true for your plans, too, A.J."

Once more Blake reached into his pocket, and this time he withdrew a small satin case. He flipped it open to reveal an antique white-gold ring with a square-cut diamond in an ornate setting.

"This was my grandmother's engagement ring. I've had it for years, waiting to give it to the woman who captured my heart and filled my life with joy. You are that woman, A.J. I never thought I could love someone as much as I love you. Before we met, I thought I was living. But I wasn't. I was just moving through my days. Life before you was like a black-and-white movie. Flat and dull and ordinary. But now it's Technicolor. And it's definitely not dull!"

He flashed her a grin, but it was forced. She could see the tension in his face, feel it in his posture.

"Believe me, I know I'm getting the better end of this deal," he continued. "But while I might not always be the most exciting guy around, I'm steady. And dependable. And I honor my commitments. So when I say that I promise to love you to the very best of my ability every day of my life, you can count on it. For always."

He closed the lid of the box, placed it in her hand, and folded her delicate fingers over it.

"I know I've thrown a lot at you and that you're scared. But I would be honored if you would accept this and become my wife. Take it with you. Think about it. Pray about it. And know that I'll be waiting, however long it takes."

He leaned toward her, and his lips brushed hers, just a momentary touch before he stood. He gave her one last, lingering look, his hand cupping her cheek. "I love you, A.J. I'll call you tomorrow." And then he was gone before she could speak.

A.J. stared after him, and a moment later she heard the bell, followed by the click of the front door. Her mind was reeling as her brain worked frantically to process everything Blake had just told her. In the end, she realized that it came down to three things. Blake loved her. He was leaving. And he wanted her to go with him, as his wife.

She glanced down at the small satin box in her palm and slowly lifted the top. The diamond winked back at her, and she traced the edges wonderingly. Blake had been saving this for a special woman all these years. For her.

A.J. drew a shaky breath and brushed her hair back from her face with trembling fingers. She'd known they were heading this way. Had been prepared to put her fears aside and take a second chance on love with this special man. But she hadn't realized that he would ask her to leave everything else behind. Yet wasn't that what love was all about? She thought about the words from the book of Ruth. "Do not ask me to abandon or forsake you! For wherever you go I will go, wherever you lodge I will lodge, your people shall be my people, and your God my God." Those were words spoken by a daughter-in-law to her mother-in-law. How much more true they should be between a man and wife.

A.J. knew that leaving St. Louis wasn't Blake's preference. He loved it here. He loved Turning Leaves. And he loved her. Yet he was willing to give up the life he'd built here over the past several years, tear up roots that went deep, because of a sense of obligation to his family and a need to reconnect with parents who had been largely lost to him. She understood that. Admired him for it. And surely she could move, too. After all, she'd only been here a few months. Her roots were still new and could easily be transplanted.

But A.J. knew it was more than that. For a few moments, before he'd proposed but after he'd told her he was leaving, she had recalled with startling clarity the sense of loss and abandonment she'd felt when Eric died. Had been vividly reminded of the reasons she'd been so afraid to commit again, to make plans for the future. Blake's proposal had quickly followed, so this time the ending had turned out differently. She was being given a choice about which direction her life took. But the next time, the choice might not be hers. If she went with Blake and built a new life with him in Oregon, she had no guarantee it would last.

Slowly A.J. closed the lid of the ring box. A wonderful man had just proposed to her. Had offered her his love and fidelity for as long as he lived. Her heart should be overflowing with joy. It was a dream come true, filled with the promise of a beautiful future.

But it was overshadowed by the nightmare of her tragic past.

And until she put that firmly to rest, until she left yesterday behind once and for all, she knew that it would be impossible to move forward and embrace tomorrow.

Blake raised himself on one elbow to glance at the digital clock by his bed. Two in the morning. He dropped back with a groan and placed his forearm on his forehead as he stared at the dark ceiling.

He'd half expected A.J. to call after he'd left the shop. But she hadn't. So finally he'd gone to bed. Which was useless. He hadn't slept more than an hour, and then only in fitful spurts.

He thought about how she'd looked when he left. Shell-shocked. Wide-eyed. Confused. It wasn't the reaction he'd always expected when he finally proposed to the woman he loved. But then, not much about their relationship had been predictable.

Was there something else he could have said? Should have said? Some other way to explain what was in his heart? Had he made it clear how much he loved her? He wasn't always the most eloquent guy, despite his love of the printed word. Even though he'd given it his best shot, he was less and less confident as the hours ticked by that he'd convinced her of the depth of his feelings. And less and less confident that she'd pull up roots again and follow him to another new place.

He hadn't wanted to press her last night. Not when he'd dropped so much on her all at once. He knew she needed time to think things through. But he also knew that if her answer was no, he wasn't going to give up. He couldn't. Because she'd become a part of him. And because he knew she loved him. They couldn't let fear rob them of tomorrow.

It might take the patience of Job to convince her of that. Not to mention racking up thousands of frequent flier miles. But if her answer was no, he would try again.

And again.

And he would keep trying, until he finally convinced her to say yes.

Because in his heart, he knew they belonged together.

Forever.

Chapter Twelve

"Hello. This is Morgan. Please leave a message and I'll return your call as soon as possible."

A.J. sighed and slowly replaced the receiver. She'd already struck out with Clare, who was having her own problems in North Carolina. Now Morgan was unavailable. She desperately needed to talk with somebody. And it was way too early in the morning to call anyone but family.

A.J. had tossed and turned all night, finally rising at 5:00 a.m. Fortunately, Trish and Nancy were scheduled for the Saturday shift, because she was in no shape—physically or mentally—to deal with customers. She poured her third cup of coffee, cradling it in her hands as the first light of dawn slowly seeped in under the window shade in her breakfast nook.

Felix padded into the room and looked up at her inquisitively. A brief smile touched her lips and she reached down and gave him a quick scratch.

"Hey, guy. Did I wake you?"

He tilted his head and wagged his tail.

"I know you need to go out. Just give me five minutes, okay?"

In response, he settled down at her feet, head on his paws. He waited patiently, but when five minutes turned into ten, he looked back up at her, this time more urgently.

"Sorry," she said, shoving aside her coffee cup and giving him another scratch. She stood and he followed her to the door, waiting eagerly while she clipped on his leash.

As they stepped outside, the unexpected mugginess of the mid-May day hit her in the face, and she hesitated. She'd heard about St. Louis's oppressive summer heat, but this early in the season? Even Felix seemed reluctant to venture out.

"Come on, boy. Let's make this fast," she told him as she started down the front steps.

He hung back, and she had to urge him with a gentle but firm tug on the leash. "Hey, this was your idea, buddy."

They headed down the street, and as they turned the corner she noticed a moving truck in the middle of the next block. A little boy was sitting on a low stone wall watching as the moving crew loaded boxes and furniture on the truck. His shoulders were hunched dejectedly, and A.J. felt a tug on her heartstrings at his obvious misery. Her step slowed as she approached him, and she stopped about ten feet away.

"Hi, there."

He looked up. She guessed he was about eight or nine, with reddish blond hair and a healthy sprinkling of freckles across his nose.

"My mom says I can't talk to strangers."

"That's a good rule. Can you talk to me if I stay back here?"

"I guess so." He eyed her skeptically, then glanced toward her feet. "What's his name?"

"Felix."

"I wish I had a dog."

"Maybe you can some day."

He shook his head dejectedly. "Mom says not for a while. We might have to move again."

"Where are you moving to?"

"Chicago."

"I used to live there."

There was a flicker of interest in his eyes. "Yeah? What's it like?"

"It's a nice place. There are lots of things to do there. It's right on a big lake, and there's an awesome aquarium."

He pulled up one knee, wrapped his arms around it and looked at her doubtfully. "If it's so great, why did you move here?"

She was momentarily taken aback by the question. "Well, my aunt gave me a bookshop. So I came down here to take care of it."

"Do you like it here?"

"Yes."

"Are you going to stay here forever?"

She stared at him. That, it seemed, was the question of the day. "I'm not sure."

"Where would you go if you left?"

"Maybe Oregon."

"My dad was from Oregon. He died when I was five. I don't remember him much."

She felt a pang in her heart. "I'm sure he was a very nice man."

"That's what Mom says. She misses him a lot sometimes."

A.J.'s chest grew tight. "It's hard when people you love die."

"Mom says Dad wouldn't want us to be sad, though. Because he's in heaven. And she says we shouldn't feel lonely, because God is always with us. And that He's watching out for us. I thought that if we moved, God might forget where we lived. But Mom says He always knows where we are. Even if we went to China, He'd know."

A.J. struggled to swallow past the lump in her throat. "Your mom is very smart."

"Yeah. So do you think you'll move to Oregon?"

"I haven't decided yet."

"Maybe you should talk to God about it. That's what I did, when Mom told me we were moving to Chicago. I felt better after that. I mean, I'm still sad about leaving St. Louis. But Chicago sounds pretty cool. And I'll be with my mom. And God will take care of us. So it'll be okay."

"Eric! Come have your breakfast!"

A.J. sent a startled glance toward the front door of the small bungalow, then looked back at the little boy. "Your name is Eric?"

"Yeah. Listen, I gotta go. Bye, Felix."

A.J. stared after him, watching until he disappeared inside. A lot of boys were named Eric, of course. But it was…almost like a sign. A message. A.J. didn't much believe in those kinds of things. But it seemed somehow more than just a coincidence that today of all days—when thoughts of her past, and her fears, were so prevalent—that she would run across a little boy named Eric. Whose absolute trust in God reminded her of another Eric, and put her own faith to shame.

Shaken, A.J. slowly headed for home. Weeks earlier, when she'd talked to Reverend Matthews about her unwillingness to make plans for the future, and her guilt over those feelings because she thought they indicated a lack of trust in the Lord, he'd reassured her that such feelings were human, that God understood. And slowly, over the past few weeks, she thought she'd worked through her issues. That surely the tentative plans she'd made for a future with Blake indicated she'd finally put her trust in the Lord.

But she'd only been fooling herself. Because last night, when she'd been thrown a curveball, she'd realized that she hadn't really surrendered her fears to the Lord. And unless she did, unless she trusted that He would be by her side no matter where she was, through both joys and sorrows, her words of faith were hollow.

Little Eric had learned that lesson. She hoped he clung to it better than she had when his faith was tested in the years ahead. But maybe it was time now for her to relearn the lesson. To be like the little children, simple and trusting in their faith.

A.J. took a deep breath and searched her heart for the words she needed.

Lord, thank you for sending that child into my life today. His simple faith has made me realize what I've known all along. That You are with us always, to the end of time. Somewhere along the way I've lost my confidence in Your presence. I've let fear overwhelm me. Even now, when a wonderful man has offered me the gift of his love, I hesitate. Because of fear. Fear that You'll call him home, as You called Eric, and leave me alone once more. Help me banish this fear so that I can appreciate this gift, accept it, and savor it. Help me also to feel Your presence in my life, to know that You will never abandon me even on my darkest days. Give me Your grace, Your guidance and Your strength. Help me to remember always that, in this changing world, three things abide. And to joyfully accept the greatest of these from the wonderful man whose presence has blessed and enriched my life.

As she ended her silent prayer, a quiet peace came over her. Deep in the recesses of her heart, she knew that the Lord had heard her plea. And she also knew that if she put her trust in Him, He would give her the courage to leave the past behind and accept a future with the wonderful man who was waiting for her answer to his proposal.

A tug on the leash pulled her up short. Felix had stopped by the steps to her apartment, while she had blindly continued on, lost in thought. He was looking up at her quizzically, his head cocked, and she smiled, her heart lighter than it had been in years.

She'd almost passed by her apartment.

But she now knew one thing with absolute certainty.

She wasn't going to pass up her second chance for love.

The phone was ringing when Blake entered the house after clocking almost enough miles to qualify for a marathon. Usually, running was a great stress reliever. Today, it had done nothing to dissipate his tension. All it had done was dehydrate him. Even though he'd left before dawn, the heat and humidity had been heavy in the air.

But his need for water was eclipsed by his need to answer the phone. It could be A.J. His already elevated pulse accelerated as he strode toward the kitchen and grabbed the receiver. "Hello."

"Blake?"

It was his mother. His pulse ratcheted up again, this time from fear.

"Is Dad okay?"

"Yes, he's fine. He's on the other line."

"I'm here, son. And doing well. But you sound winded."

Blake closed his eyes in relief and took a deep breath. "I just got in from running."

"That would explain it. Everything okay in St. Louis?"

"Yes." It was the easiest response, but he couldn't be sure that was true until he had A.J.'s answer.

"Good. Listen, son, your mom and I have been talking about your generous offer to be our business manager. You don't know how much that means to us."

"The idea of making this a real family business is like a dream come true," his mother added, her voice catching with emotion on the last word.

"But the thing is, son, this heart attack has been like a wake-up call to us. We started this business because natural food and healthy eating interested us. We never expected it to be so successful or so consuming. It just kind of snowballed on us, and before we knew it we were caught up in the momentum. It's been a great ride, don't get me wrong. And we're grateful for our success. But we never really wanted to be business tycoons. In the past few years we haven't had much time for a lot of the other things we love. Like travel. And more importantly, each other. So we've decided to sell the business."

For a moment there was silence.

"You're selling the business?" Blake repeated when he could find his voice.

"Yes. You've seen our books and our files, so you know that we've had a good offer from a company that wants to turn the business into a franchise," Jan said. "It's a perfect solution. And it will give us the time to try some other things. Over the years we've turned down a lot of speaking invitations around the country because we couldn't afford to be away from the business. Now we can accept them. And there's a publisher that's been after us to write a healthy cookbook for some time.

"We've also been asked to consider doing a syndicated newspaper column on healthy eating," his father added. "So we're actually really excited about making this change. Selling the stores will give us a good cushion for retirement and allow us to pursue these other interests. But we would definitely welcome your help and expertise in arranging the sale of the business. That's a little out of our league."

"Are you sure about this?" Blake asked slowly.

"Yes. We talked it over. And prayed about it. I have to admit, we were tempted to say yes to your offer just because we'd get to see you a lot more," his mother said wistfully.

"But we knew that was selfish," Carl added. "You have your own life to lead."

Blake frowned. "Is that the real reason you're doing this? For me?"

"Partly," his mother admitted. "But it's also for us. We really do want to go back to a less stressful lifestyle that lets us pursue our other interests."

"We hope you won't be a stranger, though, son. You know you're always welcome to visit anytime."

The undisguised emotion in his father's voice tugged at Blake's heart. "I plan to take you up on that."

He heard his mother sniffle. "It's good to have you back, Blake. We love you."

He hadn't been able to say it in person. He wasn't quite there yet. But somehow, by phone, it was easier. "I love you guys, too."

"We'll see you next week, son. Tell A.J. we said hello."

"I will."

As they hung up, his heart suddenly light, he knew he had a whole lot more than that to tell the woman he loved.

And he hoped that when she heard the news, when she knew that marrying him wouldn't turn her world upside down after all, she would feel more comfortable accepting his ring—and his heart.

A.J. pressed the doorbell for the third time, with the same result. No answer. She turned and looked up and down Blake's street. He was probably out riding his bike or running, she speculated, as she juggled the bagels and coffee she'd picked up on the way to his house. She supposed she could wait. He had to come back sooner or later. And they could always nuke the coffee. But she didn't want to wait. Now that she'd decided to accept his proposal, she was anxious to tell him immediately. She'd delayed things long enough.

She balanced the cardboard tray on top of the banister and dug in her purse for her cell phone. He might have his phone with him, she thought hopefully. It was worth a try.

Blake pulled a T-shirt over his head and flipped off the shower exhaust just in time to hear his cell phone ringing. He made a dash for it. "Hello?"

"Blake? It's A.J."

Her voice had a breathless quality, and his own breathing suddenly went haywire. "Hi? What's up?"

"I was hoping we could get together this morning."

"I'd like that. Where are you right now?"

"On your front porch. Where are you?"

He frowned and made his way to the front door. Through the peephole he saw her balancing a tray on the banister. Her back was to him, and he quietly opened the door.

"Turn around."

There was a momentary hesitation. "What?"

He grinned. "Turn around."

She did…and stopped breathing. Blake stood in the doorway, barefoot, dressed in cutoff jeans that revealed his muscular legs and a T-shirt that hugged his broad chest. His hair was damp and spiky, like he'd just stepped out of the shower. He still looked tired—but incredibly handsome. Suddenly she felt way too warm— and she knew her condition had nothing to do with the muggy humidity.

Slowly he pushed the door open. "I was in the shower, so I didn't hear you ringing. Come in."

She reached for the tray, venturing a quick glance at him as she passed. "I brought us breakfast. Shall I put it in the kitchen?"

"Sure." He closed the door. "Give me a minute while I run a comb through my hair and shave, okay?"

"Sure."

By the time he returned, A.J. had put out plates and silverware. He also noticed the satin jeweler's box sitting in the middle of the table. Blake's grin faded, and his gut clenched. This didn't look good.

"I already put some cream in your coffee," A.J. said.

"Thanks." He dropped into the chair across from her and took a fortifying sip. Then he glanced down at the satin box between them.

"There's something I'd like to tell you," he said slowly. "I had a call from my parents this morning."

Anxiety filled her eyes. "Is everything okay?"

"Yes. They just wanted to discuss business."

She expelled a relieved breath. "I've been so worried about your dad."

"Me, too. I'd like to tell you what we talked about."

"I'd like to hear it. But I have some things I'd like to tell you first."

"It might be better if…"

She laid her hand over his. "Please, Blake. I'd like to go first. While I still have the nerve." She tried to grin but couldn't quite pull it off.

Blake felt his stomach twist in knots. He didn't even try to speak. He just nodded.

A.J. took a deep breath, and when she spoke her voice was slightly uneven. "A long time ago, that day in the storeroom when I was trying to put a box on the top shelf, you told me that I didn't want to rely on anyone, and that's why I never asked for help. Well, you were right. I was afraid of getting hurt again. I've done a lot of soul-searching these past few weeks, and had more than one conversation with Reverend Matthews. Because when I thought about it honestly, I realized that my fear about commitments, about putting down roots, about letting people into my life, reflected a lack of trust in God. It was ironic, really. I'd always thought my faith was strong. And it was, in a lot of ways. But I hadn't been able to fully put my life in God's hands."

She looked down and began tearing her bagel into little pieces. "I was a lot like you, actually," she said quietly. "Because of your experience growing up, you didn't want to rely on anyone but yourself. So you methodically set out to make sure that your tomorrows were safe and that you were in control. I set out to do the same thing, in a different way and for different reasons. But the thing is, we don't even know if we have tomorrow. All we have is today. So we just need to live each day the best we can, accept the gifts that the Lord sends our way, and trust that He will be with us if things don't always work out as we plan."

She reached for the box and flipped it open. The antique diamond blinked back at them. Blake noticed that A.J.'s hands were trembling. So were his.

"Just when I started to put down roots, to take a chance on tomorrow, you asked me to marry you and to tear out those roots, to start over again in a new place. That scared me, Blake. To be honest, it still does. But you know what scares me more? Not having you in my life. Because in these past few months, as I came to recognize what a fine and wonderful man you are, I fell in love. I didn't expect it. I didn't even want it. But it happened. And I'm glad. And very, very grateful. Because my life is so much richer because of you. So, as Ruth told Naomi, wherever you go, I will go. As your wife."

Her voice broke on the last word. The tension in Blake's shoulders eased as his heart soared. He was on his feet instantly, and when he reached for her she came willingly. He gathered her in his arms, sending a silent prayer of thanks heavenward. He knew that A.J.'s decision had been a difficult one. Because while he hadn't doubted that her love for him was strong, he'd been afraid that her fear of being hurt again, of losing someone she loved, was stronger.

But her willingness to give up the life she'd created in St. Louis, as well as the shop she loved and had fought for, and follow him to a new place, illustrated the depth of her love. It was a gift he would always cherish. And now he could give her a gift as well.

He pulled back slightly, and gently traced the path of a tear down her cheek. "I didn't plan to make you cry," he said, his own voice none too steady.

"These are tears of joy, Blake."

"Well, then I have some news that may unleash a flood."

She gave him a quizzical look. "What do you mean?"

"You know that phone call I had from my parents this morning? They're selling the stores."

She stared at him blankly. "What?"

"They're selling the stores."

She frowned. "But…why?"

"They've had a good offer. And I think they figure it's time to move on. They said the heart attack was a wake-up call. They want to travel more and write a cookbook and go out on the speaking circuit. And spend more time with each other."

Slowly the implication began to dawn on A.J. "So they don't need a business manager?"

"Only long enough to oversee the sale."

"And then you'll come back?"

He cupped her face with his hands. "Forever."

"Don't promise forever," she said softly, her voice breaking.

He stroked her cheeks with his thumbs. "Forever,"

he repeated firmly. "Because our love isn't tied to earthly bonds. It will continue for always."

He reached for the ring and gently eased it out of its case. "We can have this reset if you prefer something more modern."

"I like vintage things. Remember?"

He took her trembling hand in his and eased the ring over her finger, his gaze locked on hers. "I love you, A.J. Lots of things change in this world, but I promise that my love for you won't. Through good times and bad, I'll stand by your side. You can count on me."

The ring slipped over her finger and settled into place. A.J. looked down at it. "It's a perfect fit," she said softly.

"Perfect," he repeated.

When she looked back up at him, his gaze was fixed on her, not the ring. Then he sealed their engagement with a kiss filled with tenderness, joy, enduring love and the promise of their life to come.

A.J. gave herself to the kiss. But before she completely lost herself in the magic of Blake's embrace, she sent a silent, heartfelt message heavenward to the woman whose legacy had made her happy ending possible.

"Thank you, Aunt Jo."

Epilogue

"This looks like an important letter."

A.J. glanced toward Nancy, who was sorting mail. "Why do you say that?"

"It's from a law firm."

A.J. reached for the letter and glanced at the return address. Mitchell and Peterson. Her aunt's law firm. Seth Mitchell had called her a few days earlier to remind her that the six-month period in Jo's will was over, and to find out whether her aunt's stipulation had been met. She'd happily informed him that not only had she and Blake carried through on their business partnership, they planned to make it a permanent—and much more personal—arrangement. He'd offered his congratulations and said he'd be in touch shortly. This must be the follow-up.

She ripped open the envelope and quickly scanned a brief note that was attached to another, smaller envelope.

"Ms. Williams: Your aunt asked that I forward this to you after the six-month period specified in her will. My congratulations again to you and Mr. Sullivan. I wish you great happiness."

A.J. glanced at the smaller envelope, written in her aunt's flowing hand, and addressed to both her and Blake. She went in search of him, and found him in the romance section, putting a stack of books on the shelf.

"Look at this," she said, holding the letter out to him.

He set the books down and took the envelope. After a quick glance, he looked back at her, puzzled. "This is from Jo. I recognize her handwriting. Where did you get it?"

"Her lawyer, Seth Mitchell just sent it. Go ahead and open it." She handed him a letter opener she'd brought from the back.

Blake slit the flap, and A.J. moved closer as they simultaneously read Jo's note.

My dearest A.J. and Blake, please accept my congratulations on your engagement. I am overjoyed that the two of you have fallen in love. It's what I had hoped for, you know. That was the reason for the stipulation in my will—to bring you together.

Much to our regret, Walt and I never had children. So A.J., you and your sisters have always been special to me. As I grew older, I knew that I wanted to leave each of you something of lasting value. I have always found great solace in books, and Turning Leaves helped me turn over a new leaf in my own life when Walt died. It went a long way toward filling the void his absence created. I hoped it would do the same for you, and that you would come to love it as Blake and I do. But I also wanted to leave you a more lasting legacy.

I felt the same way about you, Blake. I treasured your support and guidance these past few years, as well as your friendship. You have always held a very special place in my heart.

So I wanted to give you both the best gift of all. Namely, love. I am glad that you have found this priceless treasure as a result of my bequest.

I hope that both of you will forgive an old lady for her interference in your lives. But please understand that it was done out of love, with only the best intentions. I am delighted that the ending to your story is a happy one. May your future be bright and filled with faith and love.

A.J. and Blake finished reading the letter at almost the same time. When they glanced at each other, A.J. noted that Blake's eyes were suspiciously moist. As were hers.

"Did you have any idea?" she asked softly.

"None."

"But…how could Aunt Jo know this would happen?"

He shrugged. "She was a very insightful woman. I guess she knew us better than we knew ourselves."

A.J. put her arms around Blake's neck and gave him a teasing grin. "Maybe. But I plan to get to know you a whole lot better."

Blake put Jo's letter on the shelf beside him and then looped his arms around A.J.'s waist. "Why do I think that's exactly what Jo had in mind?" he responded with a smile.

"Then let's not disappoint her."

Blake leaned toward her, and just before his lips touched hers, A.J. caught a glimpse of the title of the new book he'd been shelving.

"The Best Gift."

Yes, she thought dreamily, that's exactly what Aunt Jo had given them.

And this time, with the Lord's help, it would last forever.

* * * * *

Dear Reader,

As I write this letter, I am in the midst of making plans for my parents' fiftieth anniversary party, and legacies are on my mind.

The dictionary defines *legacy* as a gift by will, especially of money or personal property. But a legacy doesn't have to consist of material things. Nor does it have to follow someone's departure from this earthly life. In fact, the best legacies aren't. They are living things, given daily, so that the lucky recipients find themselves richly blessed with the things that matter most. The things money can't buy.

My parents have given me such a legacy. I will be forever indebted to them for magical Christmas mornings, memorable family vacations and special moments of infinite sweetness. I am grateful to them for teaching me that it's better to give than to receive. For making *home* a word to be revered and honored. And for providing a shining illustration of what marriage is all about. Their legacy to me includes the gifts of acceptance. Laughter. Encouragement. Respect. Family. And, most especially, absolute love that is unconditional. Unlimited. Forever. That is a legacy beyond price.

In this first book of my new series for Love Inspired, SISTERS & BRIDES, Aunt Jo offers A.J. and Blake a legacy. But it is up to them to recognize it—and to have the courage to claim it. Because love doesn't always come in the form we expect. And it often requires a leap of faith. But with God's grace, with trust in His abiding presence, we can learn to overcome our fears and find our own happy endings.

Just like my mom and dad did.

Irene Hannon

Look for A.J.'s sister Clare's story
GIFT FROM THE HEART
available in July 2005
from Love Inspired Books.

Turn the page for a sneak peek...

Chapter One

"Adam, I've got Clare Randall on the phone. She says it's urgent, and she's willing to hold until you have a few minutes."

Adam stopped writing on the chart in front of him and glanced distractedly at Janice. "Clare Randall?"

"She called yesterday. I left the message on your desk."

"Do you have any idea who she is?"

"Not a clue."

Adam glanced at his watch. "Do I have a few minutes?"

"Mr. Sanders is in Room One, but he's telling Mary Beth about his fishing trip, so I expect he wouldn't mind if you take a couple of minutes. I can't speak for Mary Beth, though. Last time I went by, her eyes were starting to glaze over and she was trying to edge out the door," Janice said with a grin.

Adam chuckled. "You could relieve her."

"No way. Last time he cornered me I had to listen to a twenty-minute soliloquy about the newest hand-tied trout flies he'd discovered."

Adam chuckled again. "Okay. We'll let Mary Beth handle him this time. Go ahead and put the call through."

Adam made a few more notes on the chart, then set it aside as the phone on his desk rang. "This is Adam Wright."

"Dr. Wright, this is Clare Randall. I'm Jo Warren's great-niece. I believe you and my aunt were friends?"

"That's right."

"Well, I'm very sorry to tell you that my aunt passed away two weeks ago."

Adam felt a shock wave pass through him. He and Jo had met at church when he'd first arrived in St. Louis to do his residency, and they'd been friends ever since. Even after his move to North Carolina, they'd kept in touch. In many ways, she had become a mother figure for him, and he had always been grateful for her support and sympathetic ear. He'd had no idea she was even ill. But then, that didn't surprise him. Jo had never been one to burden others with her problems.

"Dr. Wright? Are you still there?"

He cleared his throat, but when he spoke there was a husky quality to his voice. "Yes. I'm just…shocked. I'm so sorry for your loss. Jo was a great lady."

His emotion was evident in his voice, and Clare's tone softened in response. "Yes, she was."

"What happened?"

She told him of the fast-acting cancer that had taken

Jo's life, and then offered her own condolences. It was obvious that Adam Wright had great affection for her aunt. "Did you know her well?"

"We met more than fifteen years ago, and she became a good friend. We attended the same church when I lived in St. Louis. She was a woman of deep faith. And great generosity."

Clare took a deep breath. "As a matter of fact, her generosity is the reason I'm calling you today. As you may know, Aunt Jo didn't have much family. Just me and my two sisters. And she was very generous to us in her will. However, there is a rather unusual stipulation attached to my bequest."

When Clare hesitated, Adam frowned and glanced at his watch. He had no idea what this had to do with him, and he couldn't keep Mr. Sanders waiting much longer. Nor did he want to face the wrath of Mary Beth if he didn't rescue her soon. He pulled Mr. Sanders's chart toward him and flipped it open, his attention already shifting to his next patient.

"So how can I be of assistance?" he asked.

"I understand that you have a daughter named Nicole?"

Adam's frown deepened. "Yes. What is this all about, Ms. Randall?"

Clare took a deep breath. "In order to claim my bequest, my aunt required that I act as nanny to your daughter for a period of six months, at no charge to you."

Adam's attention snapped back to the conversation. "Excuse me?"

Clare's hand tightened on the phone. "I know this

sounds off the wall, Dr. Wright. Trust me, I was shocked, too."

"But…why would Jo do such a thing?"

"I have no idea."

Adam tried to sort through the information Jo's niece had just given him. None of it made any sense—the stipulation, or this woman's willingness to go to such lengths to claim what couldn't be a large bequest. As far as he knew, Jo wasn't a wealthy woman. With her generous heart, she'd given away far more than seemed prudent to him sometimes. But maybe she'd had more assets than he knew.

Adam glanced up to find Mary Beth standing in the doorway. She nodded her head toward Room One, pointed at her watch and rolled her eyes. He got the message.

"Look, Ms. Randall, I've got to go. I have patients waiting. Give me your number and I'll get back to you."

Clare did as he asked, then suggested he call Seth Mitchell. "I'm not sure he can explain Aunt Jo's reasoning any better than I can, but at least he can verify that my offer is legitimate," she said.

"Thanks. I'll do that. I'll be back in touch shortly."

When the line went dead, Clare slowly replaced the receiver. Dr. Wright hadn't exactly been receptive to her offer. But she couldn't really blame him. She would have reacted the same way. After all, he was a doctor. He probably made more than enough money to hire any nanny he wanted. In fact, he might have one already. So why should he let a woman he didn't even know help raise his daughter, even for only six months?

Logically speaking, there were all kinds of reasons why Adam Wright could—maybe even should—turn her down. So she needed to put together a strategy in the event he declined to cooperate.

Because Clare needed Aunt Jo's legacy. Desperately. And she didn't intend to take no for an answer.

Send someone a little Inspiration this Easter with...

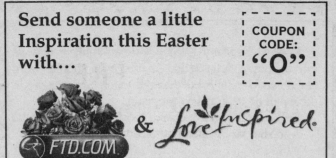

FTD.COM & *Love Inspired*

Purchase any 3 different Love Inspired titles in March 2005 and collect the coupon codes inside each book to **receive $10 off the purchase of flowers and gifts from FTD.COM!**

To take advantage of this offer, simply go to www.ftd.com/loveinspired and enter the coupon codes (in any order) from each of the 3 books! Or call 1-800-SEND-FTD and give promo code 10069.

Happy Easter from Steeple Hill Books and FTD.COM!

Steeple Hill®

Don't forget— Mother's Day is just around the corner!

Love Inspired

PAY ANOTHER VISIT TO
SWEETWATER WITH...

LIGHT IN THE STORM

BY

MARGARET DALEY

After raising her three siblings, teacher Beth Coleman
was finally free to see the world. She planned to do
mission work in South America...until a troubled teen
walked into her classroom. Beth's caring nature
wouldn't let her say no to the girl or her handsome
father, Samuel Morgan. Soon her heart was in
danger to Samuel and his ready-made family....

The Ladies of Sweetwater Lake: Like a wedding ring,
this circle of friends is never-ending.

Don't miss LIGHT IN THE STORM
On sale April 2005

Available at your favorite retail outlet.

www.SteepleHill.com   LILITSMD